Emerge

By

Lila Felix

Copyright @Lila Felix 2012
This publication is protected under the US Copyright Act of 1976 and all other applicable international, federal, state and local laws, and all rights are reserved, including resale rights: you are not allowed to give or sell this book to anyone else.
Any trademarks, service marks, product names or named features are assumed to be the property of their respective owners, and are used only for reference. There is no implied endorsement if we use one of these terms.

Editor: Jennifer Nunez

Cover Model: Miranda Reynolds

To my Husband:

I love to tell this story,

Of how you and I became us,

How me and you became we.

To those who inspire me:

Shelly C. who is probably the humblest, kindest, and most supportive person I know. She is the jelly to my peanut butter.

Amanda C. who heard this story over chimichangas and exclaimed: "You have to write that story!"

Georgia C. who made a comment that one day I needed to write a book. Big mistake girl!

Mandy A. who puts the rock in rockstar.

Gloria G. who is the sweetest of the sweet.

Thank you.

Emerge —Lila Felix

Chapter 1

    I stood outside of the house, squirming on the crumbling concrete steps trying to still my quivering heart and my nerves in preparation for what was inside. I was sweating like a pig even though it wasn't summer yet in California. My poor Chucks were losing their soles as I twisted on my toes back and forth in haste. If it was Mrs. June Cleaver waiting for me inside, I could let out that anxiety and panic in one "whoosh" of breath and enjoy the day. If it was Medusa, there was nothing I could do but to cower and jump when she said jump, trying to keep my sanity intact. I know; I'm a wuss. But I survive. I continued to stand there, cocooned in my own anxiety attack, picking at the strips of peeling white paint from the neglected side door. Maybe I could just walk really fast inside and hide for a minute. Maybe it was a good day.

    My Mom, Miranda Rouse was a complex creature, fickle to the core. She could be the Mom, or Mrs. Cleaver who cooks and cleans and acts like she cares, but always with a touch of resentment. She looks at me like she despises my very existence. She resents that I was ever born and ruined her life. She says she had so many dreams and hopes and they were all crushed when I came into her life. She claims that the only reason she actually had me was because my Dad begged her to keep me. She could also be Medusa. Medusa Mom can make you agree with her abhorrence of your existence and beg for an end to your life.

My Step-Dad, Wallace, was just ridiculously angry all the time. It was probably because he was always on pain killers or drinking beer or both. And he always complained that we never had any money for anything. But I had never seen him work, not once, ever.

They both hit. They hit each other and when that has gotten old or when they get a wild hair in their cracks, she hits me. It's like the Three Stooges reality show. It happens more often than I'd like to admit, but not often enough that I can't deal with it until I can get out of here.

I turned the stubborn and reluctant door knob and opened the door with my breath held and my stomach in knots. I had to kick the door a little bit at the bottom where the door meets the jamb to rustle it loose. I passed the laundry room, wasn't much of a room, filled floor to ceiling with laundry silently pleading to be handled.

The kitchen was small, filled with broken white cabinets and not much in the food department. It was towards the end of the month and we were out of food stamps so food was in high demand and short quantity. I would have to go to the food bank if my paycheck didn't last.

The well worn floor creaked beneath me as I snuck through the tiny kitchen and my toe caught on an upturned plastic tile. "Crap!" I whispered to myself. Unwashed dishes were in the sink from last night...not a good sign. I passed through the dining room, slowly craning my neck around the corner in search of the doom or joy which awaited me.

Through the living room, to the right, the cornflower blue carpet was halfway cleaned and the lonely vacuum stood dead center, still plugged into the wall, waiting for its master to resume the job. Again...not a good sign. But the house was quiet as I crept towards the hallway which lead to two bedrooms and a bathroom. So far, so good. I tip-toed like a cat burglar into my bedroom, which I shared with my four year old sister. We both had twin beds shoved in separate corners of the tiny room. My window had been shut. I tried to keep it open so that my sister and I didn't have to constantly smell like the nasty, cheap cigarettes my step-father chain smoked. It was those very cigarettes that were sometimes more important that electricity, more important than water, more important than his daughter eating.

Still, I heard nothing. I took the opportunity to use the bathroom in peace. It was wall to wall pink tiles, not a nice pink but that mauve-y kind of pink. It made me think of what flamingo puke might look like. I went to wash my hands, but of course we were out of soap. I managed to slide a slimy sliver from the shower and wash my hands the best I could. We were always out of some necessity...always. I stealthily snuck down the small hallway. I gained some courage and slipped my head around the corner into their room. No one was there. But the car was in the driveway.

I went through their bedroom which connected to a sun porch type room, the only way out to the backyard through the house. I carefully managed three small steps down toward a huge backyard filled with flowers and brick pathways. It was weird for people who didn't have food most of the time to have this brilliant garden. I swore that they stole plants to put in there. I heard sounds coming from the garage/office. Why people who don't work have an office was beyond me. The door flew open and it was at that moment that I knew who I was to keep company with that day. It was Medusa. I could practically see the invisible snakes rearing up and hissing at me, piled high on her head. I was surprised that my toes didn't slowly begin to turn to stone at her angry stare.

She almost flew out of the garage/office with my sister on her hip.

She said, "Jenna, ugh, finally. She has been driving me nuts all day. We are going...um...to handle some business. You'll have to watch her tonight. And get some cleaning done for God's sake."

Don't say hello or anything, I thought to myself.

But, I didn't dare say a word. If you said something to her in this state, your face might have a really quick and hard meeting with the back of her hand. But business... really? Neither one of them worked, so this must be some serious business...not. Every day that I didn't have to work, they had "business." So I took my sister and turned towards the house. They went through the gate and started the car and peeled out like there was a demon on their tails.

I turned to the sweet girl in my arms and she said, "Sissy, I'm hungry."

"Have you eaten today?" I asked her, knowing very well the answer.

She looked around to make sure they were gone...smart girl. "No."

It was almost 3:30 pm and they hadn't fed her. They probably just woke up at 1 p.m. Not unusual, but shocking all the same. The shock never seemed to wear off.

We moved to California near the end of my sophomore year for a "big financial opportunity". We intended to move in early June so that we could be settled in time for school to start. We ended up not moving until early August because...they were lazy. We stayed at grungy motel after nasty motel and were technically homeless for over six months.

We lived off of my Step-Dad's father's credit cards that he had 'borrowed' and was going to pay them off after he got a job in California. When he handed them to my Step-Father with the agreement that they were going to be paid back I wanted to shake the elderly man and call him an idiot. They were never going to get paid back. I knew it and so did they.

I didn't get enrolled in school until January and had missed an entire semester. And the only reason they did was because my real Dad had called the police and reported my truancy to them and told them where to find me. That went over well.

I made up for it the next summer in summer school but I was still angry over the whole thing. I mean, let's face it, they weren't the best kind of parents to begin with, but homelessness and truancy were all time lows for them. We finally settled in a tiny blue rental house right next to the busiest freeway in Santa Monica, California. They still had not gotten jobs but were always searching. They paid the first month and last month's rent with a cash advance from the old man's credit cards. It had been 18 months since we moved here and they were still unemployed. Not that they were ever employed before. My hope had fizzled out a long time ago.

So little May and I walked back through the house, hand in hand up the small steps into the lonely home next to the busy freeway. She was cute as a button and the very opposite of me. She had curly tendrils of blonde and the bluest eyes known to man, well, to me. I on the other hand had not wavy, but not straight brown hair with reddish highlights and these weird hazel eyes which changed colors depending on what I was wearing. We first found the bar of soap I hid in my closet in case of "soap emergencies" and headed to wash her grimy hands and face. After drying her off with a semi-clean towel, we headed to see what I could muster her to eat.

    She ended up having pork n beans with the last hot dog chopped up in it with mashed potatoes. It wasn't much, but she ate it like it was the good stuff. I washed the dishes while she ate convincing her that I ate a really good school lunch of spaghetti so she could have all of it...Even though I didn't touch that school cafeteria junk. Mostly it was the embarrassment of telling the lady in line that I got a "free lunch" that kept me from the cafeteria. I had some pride, not a lot, but some. Thankfully, the water running while I did the dishes overpowered the growling of my stomach. I finished the dishes; hers included, and cleaned up the kitchen. Then I found some necessary laundry for May and I and started a load. She went to watch a t.v. show since she couldn't watch t.v. all day with them. They didn't like to hear the kids' songs, they were annoying. They were never to be inconvenienced. Our very presence was inconvenience enough.

    I finished the vacuuming because it looked kinda strange to have one half clean and one half dirty. I put the vacuum up and made sure not to disturb the carefully hidden stack of bills that my Mom hid from my Step-Dad in the front closet. It would be her fault that they weren't paid; even though neither one of them worked. I shut the door to the closet and went to close the door to their room. *Eeewww* Their whole room smelled like a big pack of cigarettes. He'd even offered me to smoke one when I was thirteen but my Mom intervened. She had been Mrs. Cleaver that day.

May was watching Caillou as I did my homework and though I had to listen to the silliness, I didn't mind. She was content as she watched that little bald kid. I kept all A's in school, because I had to and because it distracted me from my life. I studied and paid attention in classes so that I didn't have to think about what and who awaited me at home. It was a win-win.

May had a bowl of Ramen and played outside before her bath. I made sure she was dried and in her pajamas before I went to take my shower. After I finished, I combed out my hair, brushed my teeth and looked into the face that my Mom hated. She hated the way I talked. She hated the way I looked. I had a round face, like a full moon and I was told that if I didn't wear make-up I looked like "Death warmed over." I didn't see that I was ugly, but I was not pretty either. It was awesome for my self-esteem. Once she got some random settlement check and said she was taking me to a plastic surgeon to do something about my face. Because she couldn't' stand for me to live the rest of my life 'looking like that'. She ended up spending that money on a get rich quick scam.

I did the best I could and brushed my wavy hair up into a ponytail. Then I hid my bar of soap in my closet and when I looked, May was fast asleep to the tune of some kind of dragon song. I turned off her t.v., tucked her in and went to my own corner of the room. I consoled my soul with a book about people with supernatural powers and let it be my lullaby. Later that night I heard the car come into the driveway, the doors slam, and they piled into their bed. Whew, one day down.

The next morning I woke up at 6:00 am and got ready for school. I got the clothes out of the dryer and put them on quickly. I was a jeans and t-shirt kind of girl and I didn't care if anyone liked it or not. I threw on mismatched socks and my favorite thrift store Chucks. I put concealer under my eyes and powdered my face. There, that should help with the uglies. I put some quick mascara on, grabbed my backpack and headed out the door.

I walked the four blocks to the bus stop. I swear I was the only Senior who rode the bus. I wasn't allowed to get my driver's license. My Mom was afraid that I would pull the same pranks that she did when she was a teenager. But that was ok. More time away from home. The bus driver was an elderly lady who did not enjoy driving a bus. Either that or that sour look was just her face. But she was nice enough and always winked at me when I stepped up those three steps to the front seat. The bus huffed and puffed back to life and I was officially out of my reality and into my solace. I took my book out of my bag and again used it to scab over my woes.

The day went pretty much the way most days went. I listened to the teachers, took notes, said "Hi" and "Bye" to people who sat by me. I knew people at school, but none who I would consider a friend. I was nice and smiled and pretended as Mona Lisa did. Then I remembered that I had been transferred, because of a too packed classroom, and was to endure Drama as my English substitute class. It was my last class of the day. I groaned to myself in protest, and reluctantly dragged myself into the classroom. AP Calculus and AP Physics, I could handle no problem, but Drama? Gag. Let's face it. I blushed sometimes when I said my own name.

The first person I saw was the teacher. He was an odd one. He had beady black eyes and the absolute worst looking comb-over I had ever seen. He had one of those pocket protectors in a plain white button down with khakis. He hid his beady eyes behind these overly large glasses with silver rims. He smiled at me and told me to pick any seat as he moved to greet the next student entering the class.

The windows were all open and the sun shone through the bleak classroom. The seats were in a circle and I picked one on the other side of the room. I waited for all of the other students to file in and find their seats. The teacher introduced himself as Mr. Escobar and then dramatically introduced us to what we would be doing in Drama. He didn't take roll as we were responsible to come to class and we were old enough to know that. Of course, we would be performing a play in front of the whole school...Nice. I looked around the classroom to gauge the impact of his announcement on the other students wondering if any of them shared my sentiment about the whole thing. One girl looked absolutely disgusted, one boy looked like he might puke and one boy....flatline. My lungs instantly failed me.

    This boy just looked interested and intrigued and was the most attractive guy I had ever seen in my life. He was wearing a button down navy blue shirt, rolled up at the sleeves which revealed cut forearm muscles and smooth skin. His skin was the color of caramel and cinnamon mixed together. It was brown and red simultaneously and my fingers twitched in admiration and want to run my fingers along its perimeters. On his hands was a tattoo, which curved around between his thumb and pointer finger. I couldn't read it, but it was writing...a word? He had jeans on, ripped at the knees which at the bottom overlapped a pair of burgundy Doc Martens. His knee was bouncing in eagerness or boredom, I couldn't tell, but I yearned to find out. I allowed my gaze to drift back to his face and studied his features. His hair was cropped short and jet black and met his forehead at the greatest widow's peak. He had long thick eyelashes and a goatee which even though was black, held several reddish hairs which I wanted to study closer. And his lips, God those lips...They were full and soft and it was all I could do not to leave my desk and test out those waters in front of all of these strangers.

I begged my eyes to obey and look away before I made a fool of myself, having no idea what the teacher had just said, but he was now holding some papers and handing them out to everyone. Each one was highlighted differently. What the heck? *Oh, crap, these are my lines.* I furiously turned the pages mentally calculating how much I would have to speak in this thing. Not bad, only about twenty lines. I could do this. I think. After I closed the script, smirking to myself on my lack of lines I allowed myself to glance back to the boy who still held my attention in the back of my mind only to find him smiling at me.

It was in that smile, this melt my heart, stop my breath, the world stopped turning and stood still on its axis smile, that I knew this boy would be the end of my life as I knew it and I welcomed the end. Actually, I knew he would be the beginning. His smile reached his eyes and told me so many things. It wasn't a perv smile. It was an "I adore you. I'll make you smile, too. I'll take care of you smile." It said all of the things I had never been told. It told me all the things I never dared dreaming of hearing and read about other girls hearing in books. The emotion in his eyes matched his grin and I instantly blushed and my brain swarmed with thoughts of belonging and safety and...love.

    I was snapped back to reality by literal snapping. The rest of the class was doing some kind of applause by snapping and I rolled my eyes at their theater culture. I crossed and uncrossed my legs. My blush decided to stay at full attention for the rest of the class. It was official, I was a nut job. I, apparently, had decided to test this theory out today. The class seemed to last forever but when the bell rang I was disappointed. I picked up my stuff slowly and methodically trying to time my walk out of the classroom with his. But as I looked up in the midst of my planning, he was already gone.

Chapter 2

After the bus stopped at my stop, I got off and walked the four blocks to my house. By the time I got there I was drenched with sweat and regretting not wearing shorts. I stood on those concrete steps again, silently begging God for Mrs. Cleaver. I twisted the door knob and repeated my ritual of "Guess who's in the house". There were empty grocery bags lying lonely on the counter and the dishes were done. My heart took a step back down to its resting place at the very sight. I walked through the house, braver, but not really bravely, skeptically scoping the place out. I walked through all of the rooms, the sun porch, and even the back garage/office, but there was no one there. They were gone somewhere. I just hoped they didn't lose May or forget to feed her.

I took a quick shower and got ready for my job down at the music store. It wasn't a typical music store; it was a sheet music store. It was the only sheet music store left in this city. I grabbed my messenger bag and a black sweater as it got pretty cold in that old store. I popped my earbuds in and let Better Than Ezra sing me the 12 blocks to my destination. My real Dad had bought me an iPod for Christmas last year complete with an iTunes gift card. Little did he know that it helped me keep my sanity.

My job there was simple. Vacuum the carpets then dust the furniture, clean out the practice room and re-shelve the sheet music discarded by patrons who found something bigger and better to buy. It was easy and I didn't have to talk to anyone...Which meant that no one was asking me about my life.

As the vacuum made its passes along the brown and gold shag carpet, I thought about him. You know...one of those cheesy day dreams where the guy sweeps in and breaks the vacuum in half over his knee and takes me away to a tropical beach where he professes his carnal and undying love for me. Oh man...I'm a moron. He was probably smiling at me because I had a booger hanging out of my nose or he'd never seen someone who was such a dork. He's probably sitting around his rebel hangout, leaning coolly against a motorcycle with his friends not even giving me a second thought. Who am I kidding? He never gave me a first thought.

Then I hear a snapping. *What the heck is with the snapping while I'm daydreaming?* Oh, it's the boss. Apparently there's a dusting emergency that needs my attention...stifled eye-roll. My boss is Mr. Cannon. He looks like a banjo playing, Skoal spitting, moonshine maker from Kentucky. He wears flannel all the time and calls me Little Lady.

"Well, Little Lady, it's payday, did you forget?"

Seriously, like I could forget.

"No Sir, I didn't. Do you have mine?"

"Of course I do...whatdyathink? Here it is."

He ran his words together notoriously. He did that thing where you take something back when they grab for it...Soooooooo funny. I acted very cool and casual putting it into my back pocket and resuming my job. As soon as the door hit my butt two hours later, I would be ripping it open like it was a Publisher's Clearing House check. I didn't make much, but when you don't have anything, a little is a lot and I made it stretch.

On my way home from work I was really excited. Somehow I managed to get a raise and it bumped my check up 5 bucks. 5 bucks is 5 bucks. It had gotten dark and a little cold and my thin black sweater with the hole in the elbow is not doing the job. Good thing it's only a 12 block walk. Yeah...

I walked home and let myself in...The car is still not there. Where did they go? I shrugged it off as there was nothing I could do about it. We didn't have cell phones. You had to have credit and money for that and there was no way I could get in touch with them. So I went about my business...homework and laundry. When I finished, the night had descended fully and the moon reminded me that they still weren't home. The phone had rung several times but the caller ID told me "Unknown"...That unknown lady was trouble and she loved our phone number. She was a bill collector or the IRS or somebody that didn't like us very much...I didn't blame her. Hell, I didn't like us very much. I got my book and sat on my bed by the window, curled up in my floral sheets which were pretty much worn to paper thin and waited...and waited...then fell asleep.

Six a.m. was there before I knew it and I woke with a horrendous crick in my neck from sleeping with my head perched on the windowsill. I groaned at the pain and then quieted myself for fear of waking the beasts. *Wait....did they get home?* I jerked my head around to look at the other twin bed in the corner. I pulled the sheets back in vain as I searched for the little blonde beauty. The bed was empty. I tore down the three feet long hall and looked into my parents' room. It was empty too. *They didn't come home? They didn't call? Are they ok?*

They had done this before. Once they had taken off for 4 days without notice when I was 13. It was before May was born and I didn't know what to do. I called my real Dad and he came to get me and when they got home, 3 days later, they called him and said there was an emergency and they couldn't wait for me to get home from school before they left. It was a load of crap and everyone knew it, but he brought me back home anyway. He didn't want custody of me, mostly because he thought I had a good life with my Mom and I was too chicken to tell him otherwise. The day I was returned I was greeted with spit in my face coupled with a slap to make sure I got the point. When I asked where they were, she clocked me in the jaw. All of my clothes were taken except one pair of jeans and a raggedy shirt. I was made fun of for weeks because I wore the same thing to school every day for a month straight.

Not knowing what else to do…I went to school dutifully. My classes were a haze as my brain conjured up all of the awful things that could be happening to May. I slothfully made my way into the desk in the corner of Drama. The teacher was out that day and we were told to study independently for the period. I opened up my Physics book and stared at the book, pretending to study. I was so knee deep in my worry that I didn't even notice him until the period was almost over. He was sitting three seats up and to the right of me and was lazily glancing over his shoulder, silently begging my gaze. He was wearing a white t-shirt and some dark jeans and the same Doc Martens. My eyes locked with him and it was as if he could see through me. His face reflected the worry I felt and I wondered why he looked like he cared. Was he worried about me? Did he see the worry in me and felt sorry for the poor dorky girl? At the moment, I didn't care which one it was. I found solace in his stare until it was broken by the 'not so subtle' "Aheeeemmmm" from the substitute teacher. I saw a corner of those gorgeous lips turn upward in a smirk and then they returned downward as he turned back around in his seat.

As I made my way back home after a sweet "Are you ok?" from the bus driver, I stopped frozen in my tracks as my eyes surveyed the damage. The doors to the car were wide open and the sad white backdoor to the house was marred with a shattered window. My Mom's purse lay halfway out the doorway as if it were crawling out of the house to safety. Its meager contents were lying in the aftermath. *Oh God, what happened? Please let it be ok.* I picked up the purse and its belongings, shut the doors to the car and walked into the house and set her purse on the dryer.

The kitchen cabinets were all opened and cans and boxes littered the counters and the floor. It was like an episode of "The Haunting" where the lady turns from the kitchen to put something in the refrigerator and when she turns back, all of her cabinets are open and she flips out and screams and demands they move out immediately. I stepped through and over the mess of more purse contents and cans and boxes and came upon my answer. My Mom was sitting at the dining room table, holding a cup of coffee like it was her life jacket. The right side of her face was swollen and blood trickled from the side of her mouth. She pointed to a bag of frozen peas on the table, wrapped in a kitchen towel and sobbed as she whispered "They melted." I dropped my bag and got her a half full bag of chopped mixed vegetables from the freezer and smacked it on the counter to break them from their frozen block shape. I wrapped them in the kitchen towel and said, "Here. Where's May?" Her eyes bulged and she said, "Shhhhh!!!! He's asleep." He was passed out again after a drunken tirade. I knew it. I rushed quietly to our bedroom and she wasn't in her bed. I checked the next logical place, the closet. Relief flooded my system. She was there, curled up in my thrift store hooded sweat shirt asleep from fear or crying. I left her there as I didn't know for sure if the tyrant was down for the night or just a nap. There was no telling. I shut the closet door and made my way back to the kitchen.

    I didn't ask where they had been and I didn't really care. I would get the story from May the next time we were alone and from her it would be the truth. That kid didn't lie, even though we were constantly smothered with deceit. I picked up the cans and boxes like a ninja. I was skilled at cleaning up the aftermath in silence. I saw my Mom fumble in her "secret closet" through bottles until she found her pleasure. Who knows what it was. The doctors said she was bipolar, but instead of taking the medicine on schedule she waited until she was a wreck and nearly overdosed herself with whatever concoction she fancied. I shut the cabinets and the last one gave a cry of pain as it shut. I stopped to listen, seeing if the whiny cabinet woke him, but didn't hear anything. By this time it was dark and I gathered a blanket, my pillow, a flashlight and my book and made my way to the closet. I wasn't even going to bother with homework or showering tonight for that matter. I was safe for tonight and so was May. The last thing I thought about before going to sleep was that almost smirk from the boy who I wished was mine.

Chapter 3

If my Mom thought I was ugly on a normal day, she would have called the ugly police on me this morning. The dark bags under my eyes were big enough to hold a small child. I looked like Voldemort on a bad day. I did what I could, got dressed, and made my way to school. Before I left, I put May in my bed and tucked her in. She would get in trouble if she was caught sleeping in the closet. At least she was home safe and as twisted as it sounds I was grateful for the fight last night. It meant I didn't have to anticipate one for a good while. I could breathe easy for a month at least, maybe 6 weeks if my Mom was extra submissive and daunting on him. He would spend the day apologizing and fake blubbering how much he loved her. I hate the blubbering. I was once again grateful for school.

I hadn't eaten the day before and my stomach gave me a sharp reminder as I passed the heavenly smells of the bakery which was right next to school. I stopped in and scrounged change for a glazed donut. I downed it like a hyena and then quenched my thirst at a water fountain in the first hall I could get to. I was still hungry, but oh, well. I made my way to Homeroom, grateful for my routine.

Later, I was walking through the Science Hall after third period Calculus and trying not to be tardy to Physics when I saw him. It was the first time I had seen him out of Drama class and I did a double take as if I didn't believe he existed outside of sixth period. He smiled that perfect smile at me and I gave him a stupefied tight lipped smile that I usually give freely to strangers and the lady at the library. *It's official, I'm a dork.* I was contemplating giving myself a good smack against the concrete wall when I heard it. "Carlos, wait up man!!" Instinctively, I turned around, somehow knowing that it was him they were calling to. He turned and greeted the other guy and they assumed their walking. *Carlos...Holy crap, that's his name.* It was just his name, but somehow it was a new, though small, something I knew about him.

Time never goes fast when you want it to. And today was no exception. Fourth and fifth periods seemed longer than my whole day. I rushed out of fifth period AP American History and walk-ran the distance down the stairs to Drama class. My messenger bag was literally kicking my butt all the way down. Once I reached the second flight of stairs I slowed to a snail pace, trying to look calm and cool walking to class. Yeah, when you have to pretend to be calm and cool walking to class you know you're a grade 'A' turd basket. I took a deep breath and entered the classroom sauntering along like I wasn't jonesing to see him. *Calm down Moron, you're gonna have a panic attack. You're probably foaming at the mouth or something. Even if you see him, all he sees is a pity case or an ugly duckling.*

I walked in and took a seat in the back, not because I like to sit in the back, but it was the only seat that had an empty seat next to it. "I Wuz Here" was carved into the top corner of the surface. Had to be the work of a genius, right? I scanned the class looking for him while pulling out my script for the play. Moron clue #2, looking around a classroom for a boy while you pull papers out of your backpack at .23 mph. I rolled my eyes at myself and steadied my breath. The tardy bell rang and sadness crept in. He wasn't here today. I resolved to being a bit sad. Then the door opened and I swear I heard "Howl" by Florence + The Machine playing around me. He was there and he was eyeing the seat next to me.

He walked in and slipped casually into the seat next to me. I got the feeling that everything he did was smooth. Today we were supposed to talk about costumes and stage directions and other theatrical things. But in the 2 feet that separated me from him there was this heat wave, kinda like the waves of heat that emanate from a space heater. I could almost hear the hum of it and I blushed furiously at the thought that he felt it too. Then that wench Real World got my attention. *There's no way this guy feels what I feel for him. There's just no way. He's not attracted to me. I'm just me. I might as well be an Amish wallflower.*

Out of the corner of my eye I could see him studying his lines, really intently. I had probably stared at him through my peripheral vision for forty minutes. Someone knocked at the door and the teacher excused himself for a minute.

As soon as the door closed he turned to me, still in his desk.

"Hey," he said.

"Hi," I croaked out.

After an awkward minute he added, "So...you weren't in this class last semester."

I hesitated and then answered, "No...I was in Senior English, but it was full this semester because that one teacher quit so they put me here."

It was like the words were coming out and my brain was letting them through the gate without any censorship.

He smiled, and said, "Well, that makes it easier." I shook my head trying to jumble the words into place in my head.

I answered, "Makes what..."

The bell blared in my ears causing me to look up at the clock and when I turned back to the conversation he was gone.

The whole bus ride and walk home was spent overanalyzing his statement. *What did he mean? Why did he say that? Was he talking about me or the class? So, he noticed I wasn't in that class last semester or he just noticed I was a new student this semester?*

I analyzed it and ran it over in my brain until I had caused a two minute conversation to become a two hour throbbing headache. But that two minute conversation had made my day, my week, maybe even my year. I caught a glance at my house as I walked under the freeway overpass and cringed. *Here we go again.*

Chapter 4

The house was clean and dinner was made when I got home which was typical after a big Tyrant episode. Later I would find out from May in a middle of the night closet conversation that Mom and the Tyrant had gotten some 'big money." That's what May called it. She was extremely smart and listened to everything then repeated it back like a parrot.

It was probably one of their famous random settlement checks for $2,300 or some other odd amount and they went to a local casino to double it. They were always suing people and this was one of their paydays. Of course they lost it all, hence the Tyrant episode. It was my Mom's fault they had lost all of the money.

May had been left with some lady that Mom had only talked to twice but apparently she was really nice to her and made what May called "sprinkly brownies". And apparently that lady had given Mom quite the talking to about something outside, but May couldn't hear what they were saying.

I had worked that day, only for two hours and Mr. Cannon cashed my paycheck that I still had folded up from the day before yesterday. It was $213.36 and I was hoarding it in case the groceries Mom bought with her mysterious check didn't last. I needed stuff, but I could deal without until I knew we were in the green.

Mom was Mrs. Cleaver again and not by choice, but to keep the peace. She ran through the house towards his room frantically every time he screamed "Miranda!" Her bruises were fading already but she still flinched when she smiled her fake smile. She would always make three square meals and keep the house neat as a pin after a big Tyrant event. She would keep this routine up for about a week and then it would slowly deteriorate into Medusa/Mrs. Cleaver whiplash.

So I woke up the next day in a great mood and even put a little extra effort into my make-up and hair. I wore it down today since it was fairly cool out and it wouldn't catch the frizzies. It was long, passed my shoulder blades but still that same brownish color. I shrugged at my reflection and grabbed my bag. I put a hair band on my wrist just in case.

I made myself pay attention in my classes and prayed that it would make the time go faster. I was itching for just one look at him. It really does wonders to pay attention when the teacher is....you know...teaching. I found myself unaware that it was time for the bell, class after class. But I was hyper aware of the clock during fifth period. I wanted to get into Drama class so bad that I was tempted to clothesline my fellow students as they passed to make the hallways less crowded.

I walked into class and he was there. Carlos....he was there sitting at his desk methodically rubbing the bridge of his nose between his forefinger and thumb. He looked tired or stressed and I wondered what a guy like him had to stress about. I sat in the only desk available, the one behind him even though I had plowed through the halls trying to get there early. He didn't notice me walk in and I was too much of a coward to say anything to him. The Drama teacher wasn't in class...again...and we were told to study on our own. So I did.

I studied the back of his head and memorized the hairline which threatened to go into his collar and my fingers twitched in want of reaching out to touch him. I longed to find out what he smelled like. I wanted to wrap my arms around that neck and push my face into his neck while he told me why he was stressed. I closed my eyes instantaneously and rattled the thoughts out of my head. *Get over yourself, Jenna....as if.* I instead opened my latest reading conquest and began to lose myself in the tale of a wolf-man and his mate.

After a while, I looked up as movement caught my eye in front of me. That same guy from the hallway, who tipped me off to Carlos' name, was giving him crazy eyes like he was watching Wimbledon on a big screen TV. After a minute his tennis eyes took over his head and he began bobbing it, towards my way. I wondered if there was a girl behind me who they thought was hot or he had a violent twitch. I glanced back to see who it was so I could berate myself mentally for not looking more like her. I didn't see any girls behind me and so I resumed being entranced by the wolf claiming his mate. My book was pushed slightly and suddenly I was face to face with *him*. He was turned around towards his left and looking over my book at me.

"Hi, Jenna," he said with a voice that curled my toes in the security of my Chucks.

"Oh, hi..."

I tried to be so cool. I sounded like a prairie dog on crack.

"You know my name?" I said.

"Um...yeah...Mr. Escobar said your name when he was giving out the parts in the play."

"Oh, yeah..."

I rolled my eyes at myself just wallowing in my stupidity.

"So..." he smiled, "have you learned your lines yet?"

I half smiled back, " Nah, I don't have many so I really haven't started yet."

He chuckled a little at that and added "Well, next week we start practicing in the theater every class so you should learn them."

"Yeah," I said, "I'll do that."

"It will be nice to see you somewhere out of this classroom."

As he spoke I noticed for the first time that today he had dark circles under his eyes and he looked exhausted. I wondered why, but again, I was too much of a chicken to ask. He turned back around while I was still in La-La Land and I resumed reading until the bell rang. As he got his backpack to leave he turned around and gave me a look that stilled my heart. He gently tugged at the end of one of my brown strands of hair.

"By the way, your hair looks pretty like that."

He said this and then made a quick exit with the other students. He just left. *Note to self: Never put your hair up again....ever.* It took me at least a minute to be able to move again to catch the bus.

The next day was more of the same conversation as the day before and I cringed at the thought of practicing in the theater on Monday and of not seeing Carlos for two days. The weekend went off without a hitch as Mr. Tyrant and Mrs. Cleaver were still playing nice and had even let May watch some TV. I worked for twelve hours on Saturday. Mr. Cannon said I could because the place was swamped. I never thought a sheet music store could be swamped, but it was really busy. I was glad for it. It got me out of the house and hooked me up with a sweet paycheck. And while I worked I daydreamed of the boy with caramel and cinnamon skin who made me want to find a home in his arms and let his heartbeat soothe my battered mind.

Chapter 5

The next month came and went with side glances and smiles and simple small conversation. He laughed at my goofy jokes and I hung on to his every word. I was asked by several of the girls in Drama class if I liked him. Whether or not he had asked me out. Whether or not he liked me. I blushed when I was asked if I liked him and my rose red cheeks gave the answer that my mouth could not bear to give. I truly didn't know if he was into me or not. If I had to go only by his glances or his smile I would say "yes." But if I had to go by actions, I wouldn't know the answer. He often lent a hand to help me up when we were all sitting around and he opened the door for me, but he hadn't asked for my phone number and he hadn't asked me out. Maybe he had a girlfriend. The very thought turned my stomach.

Home was like a bad episode of the Twilight Zone. Something dramatic had changed during that last episode between the Tyrant and my Mom. I wish I knew what it was so I could keep it in my pocket for the future, but I didn't know. She was keeping the house fairly clean and hadn't traded any of our food stamps for cigarette money yet this month. Food was cooked and she even enrolled May in a preschool and was taking her every day. It was some kind of income based preschool and of course we qualified because there was no income.

I had found out that our rent was being paid by a different relative every month. It used to be paid by my Dad, but as soon as I turned 18, my child support checks had stopped. I know my Step-Dad's relatives thought they were helping, but they were just allowing them to remain unemployed. Neither one of them were speaking to me and I didn't speak to them for fear of spooking them out of their "happy little family" routine. May was coming out of her shell and I was beginning to lose the fear that I would never be able to leave home because I needed to protect her. Maybe she would be ok. Maybe they would take care of her.

Going to the theater instead of the classroom became routine and something I looked forward to; even though nothing significant had happened. It was the last Friday before the performances which were scheduled for Wednesday, Thursday and Friday. It made me nauseated to think about an actual crowd filling these lonely seats. I went from the sunshine day to the dark of the theater and was temporarily blinded by the dark. I walked past the first row of theater seats and inhaled the muggy old scent of the theater. I chucked my messenger bag onto one of the seats in the second row and made my way to the dressing room to help some of the other girls with their make-up. I had helped Anna with her gaudy "girl gets around town" make-up for her character and walked out onto the stage for a breather.

I sat on the edge of the stage on what I had learned was stage right near the curtains and swung my legs over the edge. I watched as the students on the stage to my left rehearsed with dramatic flair as the mother in the play did not approve of her son marrying that ho-bag. I looked out over the theater seats and then I heard the theater doors open to my left. The sun from outside made me put my hand up above my brow to help me see. What I saw next caused my stomach to do more tumbles than a gymnast on meth. It was Carlos, dressed in a button down shirt with his trademark sleeves rolled up to his elbows wearing brown boots and scruffy jeans. He had a leather wrist band on today, but it was what was on the other arm, or should I say hip that instantly smashed my heart and confirmed my doubts.

On his hip was the loveliest baby I had ever seen and on the other side of that baby was a petite pretty Hispanic girl, our age, with long black hair, holding the baby's hand. I had seen her before at school. She was in my homeroom during her pregnancy and had stopped coming near the end. I never saw her with a guy. The inner dialogue began, my cheeks turned to flame and my pretzels I had eaten for lunch taunted and threatened to make themselves known by coming up through my throat. *That's a baby. It's his baby. Oh God, that's his girlfriend or wife and his baby. He has a baby! You are a home-*

wrecker. I can't believe you thought he liked you. Why would he when he already has her? He has a baby! What the hell were you thinking? You are living in a state of delusion! Moron alert!

I thought these things as I pushed up off of the stage and made a bee-line through the blood red, heavy curtains and pulled them right and left in a panic to hide. I finally reached the girls' dressing room and closed the door behind me and sat on the nearest thing, which was an ancient space heater attached underneath the window. I could hear my heart beating in my ears and looked around to see if anyone could hear it too. This was the first time I had ever begged for the clock to end Drama class for the day. A girl who had previously asked me about Carlos came in suddenly, closing the door behind her and was a bit out of breath.

"Did you see that," she huffed.

"Which part, the girlfriend or the baby?" I spat at her.

My fear and hurt had quickly turned into frustration and anger. The anger protected me when I needed it. And I needed it now.

She then puffed, "But that's Natalie. I've seen her with another guy and I could've sworn they were together."

Huff, huff, puff... "Maybe we are misunderstanding."

But I had made up my mind.

"Well, I'm not sticking around to find out."

"Can you go get my bag for me?" I begged her.

She came back quickly, still gasping for air and handed me my bag.

"Thanks," I whispered. She began to protest.

"But, Jenna.."

I threw up my hand to make her stop. I grabbed my bag and for the first time ever I skipped class and left school early. I ducked out through the back of the theater and through a hole in the outside gate that I had heard the other kids talking about and freed myself from school and from the thoughts of him.

I caught the public bus closest to school and took the scenic route back home so I would arrive home around the same time as usual so I didn't trip up Mom. Not that they cared. Hell, they were still not speaking to me. I cried on the bus...cried until I was cried dry. By the time I made it home I was numb from head to toe. I walked through the kitchen, through the now clean house, collapsed and let my sleep take away my thoughts. No one had spoken to me on my way to my bed and no one asked if I was ok.

Chapter 6

The weekend was long, and it was exactly the way I wanted it. I wanted it to drag out forever and for Monday to never come. I know everybody wishes that the weekend would last forever and it was a first that I agreed. But Monday came and I slothed out of bed, now determined not to let this boy get me down. I justified it in my head. *He just smiled and complimented your hair, Idiot. He didn't profess his love or give you a ring. What are you? Some lovesick little girl who's gonna cry just because he's already taken? Just because you'll never be enveloped in his arms? Just because you thought you could be safe with him? Just because you yearn to feel his hands on you? Ok, ok, stop already.*

That useless little pep talk got me all the way through the day until fifth period ended and then I was back to hating Drama, the class and the experience. It was all I could do to make my feet walk the path that I knew would take me back to where he was…Where I saw him with her. I walked through the Science building, taking a detour to the theater. I stepped out of the Science building determined to hold my head up high. I walked pointedly towards the theater doors and when I went to open them a strong, warm, calloused hand grabbed my elbow. "Jenna, please wait," he said.

I stared through the crack of the open theater door as it slowly shut before me. I was so close to it that I wondered if it was going to catch on the tip of my nose as it passed. And I kept staring until it was fully closed. I knew who was talking to me. I think I would recognize his voice in a sea of people at a rock concert. I took two deep breaths before I turned to face him.

"What?" I asked with a smile so fake it couldn't be rivaled by Barbie herself.

"I wanted to talk to you," he nervously said as he put his hands into his pockets and rocked back and forth on his heels.

"Me? Why?" I asked.

He huffed out a slow breath and let it out again. His thumbs were in his front pockets and he was shuffling his feet in the rocks on the ground.

"Can we talk over here?" he asked as he pointed towards a bench which had been tagged with random graffiti.

I looked around in anticipation at what he wanted to say.

"Yeah," I answered and sat down, stiff as a board on the dilapidated bench.

"I'm sorry if you got the wrong idea on Friday. I saw your face when I walked in, but..."

He looked me straight in the eye and I could see the honesty through his. But I was still feeling snarky.

"I think I got the idea loud and clear. And I'm glad for you. She's a beautiful baby."

I had decided midway that I wanted to take the high road.

"Well..." he started, "she is a beautiful baby, and Natalie is one of my closest friends."

"That's great. You looked happy."

Oh, this high road thing was really starting to suck.

"Yeah, I never thought being a Godparent would be so much fun. But Caroline is great."

I stumbled in my logic, in my emotions and in my speech.

"Godparent?" I whispered, quietly begging for this to be true.

He chuckled that long slow delicious chuckle and chastised

"Yeah, what'd you think?"

I blushed with such force that I was sure a satellite could've picked up the hue.

"Um...well...."

He reached out and touched my arm right above my wrist and slowly moved it down to settle on the side of my hand.

"I'm so sorry. I should've said something before, but Natalie wanted to meet you and she had brought the baby to school to see all of her friends and... I didn't think."

I didn't know what to say. We weren't together. Why was he apologizing? I was so completely embarrassed.

"I'm sorry too. I assumed...I mean I saw you and I thought...I shouldn't have..."

He was holding my hand now. Stroking the outside of my hand with his thumb back and forth. Were his hands really warm or were mine really cold? I didn't really care which.

"It's ok. Now you know. And there's something else you should know."

Surely my sternum was going to crack any moment. I mean..my heart thumping was ridiculous.

"What?" I said it all breathy, it sounded like I was trying to be a girl on a '1-900 talk to a skank' commercial.

"I think you're smart and you..." He took a deep breath and bounced his knee a bit, but he never let go of my hand.

"Jenna, I think you're beautiful and well...can we go out sometime? I would love to get to know you."

My answer came out before I could even think it over.

"Yeah."

He smiled...oh, that smile. All of my stress and worry about him and that girl and that baby was gone in an instant and what he felt about me was confirmed in that conversation and in that smile. We sat staring at each other for who knows how long and then made our way into the theater. We practiced and went through the plays as if we had a packed house. Some people still didn't know their lines and I still sucked at mine but it was going to be ok. The deal was, you participate in the play, you get an 'A'.

After class was over, I gathered my bag and my sweater and made my way towards the doors to catch the bus, and a hand intertwined with mine and a wave of heat crept up my body starting with the hand that was held so dearly.

"Didn't we forget something?" he asked.

I could think of tons of things that we didn't do that I wanted to do with him or to him, but I said, "We did?"

He smiled and said, "Yeah, I didn't get your phone number."

"Oh" I smiled and tried not to let on what I was really thinking about.

Would they even let me talk on the phone? Would I have any privacy? What if he calls and they answer and give him a hard time? I put those thoughts on the backburner and took a pen from my bag.

"Here." I turned his hand over to write my number on it and he stopped me.

"No, I have to go to work tonight and it will wear off. Write it on my notebook. Here"

He handed me a blue spiral bound notebook. I did as he asked and then questioned him.

"You work at night?"

He nodded and said, "Yeah, my brother and I live in an apartment together and so I have to work"

I nodded and said, "I understand. Well, I have to catch the bus, so I will see you tomorrow, ok?"

I was having a hard time letting go of his hand. Our fingertips were still touching as we walked away and he said, "Ok, tomorrow."

I made myself face forward and not look back as I walked away but hoped that he had glanced back.

I made it home but there was no one there. A note was left on the window of the backdoor that was now sported duct tape instead of glass. *Jenna, we are going to visit your Aunt Catherine for a few days. We left food in the fridge.* That was it. No "I love you" or "Kiss my butt" or anything. Aunt Catherine lived in Las Vegas so it was about 8 hours away. It was actually a relief now. Ever since that trip where they lost all of their money my Mom was being a Mom. Well, she was being a Mom to May and that's all I cared about. I walked into the house and was glad for the silence. I could wait out his call knowing I was free to talk to him without prying eyes or ears.

So, then I played that game where you pretend you're not waiting for someone to call. I cleaned, I did homework, I read, I showered and made dinner. And by the time I was elbow deep in dish water, the phone rang. I ran with the dish rag still drying my hands to the ringing. I checked the caller id and it was a local number that I didn't know.

I answered, giving the caller my best suave, "Hello".

"Hey," the baritone voice answered. "It's me. I'm sorry. I hope it's not too late to call."

I was so excited that I had twisted that poor dish rag until it wouldn't twist any more.

"No, it's fine. I stay up pretty late." I giggled. *God, I'm losing it. Why was I giggling? Nothing was funny.*

"Oh, good. I'm on my lunch break," he said, sounding relieved.

"Oh, well shouldn't you be eating? I mean…I'm glad you called but I don't want you not to eat."

He laughed into the phone. "No, I don't eat when I'm here. It's too late to eat. It makes me tired."

Poor guy, it was obvious to me why he was looking so tired the other day. He was exhausted from going to school all day and then working all night.

"That makes sense," I said, not knowing what else to say.

"So, what are you doing tonight?" he asked. He sounded like he'd never done this before.

"Well, I did some homework and cleaned up and did some laundry."

He laughed again. "Yeah, I probably should do laundry too."

I replied, "Well, if I don't do it then no one does. But I've done it for years, so it's no biggie."

He paused a little too long. "You don't live with your parents?"

"Yeah, I do, but I kinda have to take care of myself."

"Oh..." He sounded...Worried? Concerned?

"So, how long do you work every day?"

He explained and the rest of our first conversation was easy and familiar.

I didn't realize how long we had talked and then he let out an enormously long breath and said "I don't want to, but I have to go back to work. I will see you tomorrow, ok?"

"Um, yeah, ok." I didn't want to hang up.

"Ok, well, bye."

"Yeah, ok, bye."

I hung up first. He needed to get back to work and I didn't want to be the reason he got in trouble.

I know it was just a phone conversation, but I felt like I knew some things about him that no one else did...Like we had secrets. I put the phone back where it belonged and danced the twirly ballet of a girl who had just talked to the boy she adored. I was no ballerina, but I twirled and twirled.

Chapter 7

I woke up the next morning in the greatest mood. I was still by myself in the house and I got up and took the time to make myself a grape Pop Tart in the toaster. High class breakfast. I dressed in a pair of ratty jeans and a black and white striped Henley and my black garage sale Mary Jane's. I braided my hair over the side of my face even though I swore I would wear it down every day because he said it looked pretty. *Who am I kidding?* I hardly ever wore my hair down. I wore my usual minimum make-up and glided to the bus stop. Nothing in the world could bring me down from this. Nothing.

The day went by and as I made my way, in a haze, through the halls between third and fourth periods, I saw him walking down the hall. I pretended to look straight ahead, determined not to be that girl that came unglued at the very sight of him. But in my peripheral I spotted him and he had spotted me. He didn't say anything as he passed; the hallways were two 'moos' away from a cattle drive in between classes. Instead, he reached out his finger and ran it down my arm as slowly as he could while never missing a beat. I gasped as that simple touch caused pins and needles to crawl up my arm and spread through my body. I turned my head quickly around to verify what had just happened and he was glancing back at me too. He was smiling the smile of "Ha! I got you to blush!" It was true and that small gesture and the heat that proceeded lasted me through until the coveted sixth period arrived.

Leaving fifth period in and of itself caused my blush to come to full attention. I turned and situated my messenger bag across my chest and began to walk towards my destination. As I crossed campus and passed by the English building someone took pace with me and then I knew who it was. I pursed my lips together to keep from smiling like a serial killer clown.

Fingertips teased and taunted mine, playing my fingertips like the keys of a piano. Then he nudged my shoulder with his, trying to get my attention. Little did he know that he had my attention every single second and his playful gesture caused warm tingles to spread up my arm and throughout my body. I looked over at him and he had a different smile. It was a new smile. It was a smile that conveyed my thoughts to a T. We had a secret that no one else knew. And I had a secret of my own...I wasn't willing to admit it in words, but it was there nonetheless. The thought itself shocked me like a bolt of lightning. It was too fast and it didn't make sense and I hardly knew what loving someone was. I chastised myself for being a fool. But I knew what love wasn't and I knew how love didn't act and things that love didn't do and I knew how his very presence made me feel.

We reached the theater and he held the theater doors open for me. I smiled bashfully at his gesture and as I walked in he placed his hand on the small of my back and caressed it gently, testing out the waters. I turned slightly and looked at him over my shoulder as the door closed and slightly nodded giving my permission. As we walked towards the class, who were all perched in various positions on the stage, I caught Anna's eye and knew by the way she was covering her smile with her hand that she knew what was going on. We walked, Carlos still behind me up the small stairs towards the stage and plopped down next to each other. I'm sure Mr. Escobar was talking about something really interesting, but what it was I knew not. I caught the end of his pep talk and heard how we were ready and it was going to be great. We were to spend the rest of the class studying our lines and after that we could do what we wanted to do.

When I got up Carlos was talking to that Wimbledon head bobbing guy and I made my way into the audience seats towards the middle on stage left. Students had made small groups all around studying their lines, or pretending to. And that is exactly what I was doing. As I entered the row to take a seat, my shoes made a ridiculous noise as they were sticking with every step. Theaters are always sticky. I decided on the third seat in as to not bring any more attention to me and my sticky steps. I pulled out my script and wrapped it around the outside of my trusty paperback. The wolf-man's mate had been kidnapped and I needed to know more. About ten minutes later the seat next to me was pushed down by a hand with cinnamon skin and he sat down slowly, like he was gauging whether or not he was welcome. I put my head back against the seat and turned towards him and smiled, hoping that would give him the answer he needed.

"You don't have your script," I said. "You're not very good at fooling the teacher."

He laughed and responded, "I'm not trying to. He said we could do what we wanted to if we already knew our lines. What I want to do is talk to you."

All I could muster up was, "Oh."

He looked around the room. I didn't know if he was bored or thinking of something to say. All of the sudden my cowardly lion got courage.

"I enjoyed talking to you last night." He leaned his head back and mimicked me by turning his head towards mine.

He agreed with a whisper. "Yeah, me, too. Are you gonna be home tonight?"

Was he still nervous around me? Didn't he know what I would give to talk to him again?

"I have to work from 4-6:30, but I should be home after that. You go on break at 7, right?"

He smiled and said, "No, I'm off today and tomorrow."

I was happy about that not because he would call me but because again today he looked absolutely spent, like he was running on fumes. I found myself caring whether or not he was working too much and glad that he was going to get to rest.

"That's good. You...well...you look tired."

He smiled that gorgeous smile. "Is that your way of telling me I look like crap?"

I jolted up and words just started coming out of my mouth. It probably sounded like a rabid squirrel but I couldn't let him think that.

"No, that's not what I meant. I mean you must be tired going to school all day and working all night. And I would be exhausted and sometimes you just look like you're tired. You don't look bad, the opposite in fact. I mean you know you're...you know...look at you. But I just meant that I know you must not get much sleep and.."

I was stopped and shocked into a state of calm when his hand suddenly enveloped mine with the briefest of moments. I pleaded with him in my mind. *Don't stop. Don't let go.*

"It's fine. I was just kidding. You should've seen your face."

I flounced back in my seat and groaned in defeat. But he soon went back to his serious face.

"And yeah...I do get tired. Sometimes it seems like I can't go another minute but I have to. So, what about you? Where do you work?"

We talked for the rest of the period about work, parents, school, and everything in between. The time flew and before I knew it the rest of the class was filing out towards the door.

"We better go. They lock the theater up in the afternoons," he said.

He read my mind. I was tempted to stay here all day.

"Yeah...I guess we better."

I made my feet move after we had left the theater towards the bus and I looked back to say goodbye and he was right behind me. Our bodies brushed together as I turned and every part of my body became an erogenous zone all at once. I let out a yelp that could best be described as Minnie Mouse watching a horror movie.

He tried to mask his laughter by clearing his throat and said, "You forgot your bag."

I rolled my eyes at my own ignorance and he stepped closer to me and placed the strap onto my shoulder. He was so dang close. That was the first time I really noticed the way he smelled. The scent was all male and it was like Aspen trees and cinnamon mixed together. *Oh, to camp in that forest.* That was the best description I could come up with. I inhaled it as deeply as I could, trying to make that smell permanently stick to the inside of my nose. I closed my eyes momentarily and let the sensation overwhelm me. His face was inches from mine...Inches. He had a peppermint in his mouth and I could smell it as he spoke to me.

"Can I take you home?" he asked as his eyes never left mine.

I panicked a little at the thought of my nut-jobs, I mean parents, being home, but then remembered they were still gone.

"You don't mind?" He grinned and tipped his head forward so that our foreheads met.

"Of course not." He shook his head a little as if exasperated with me.

"Come on."

He took my bag back and piled it on his shoulder on top of his own and nodded his head towards the student parking lot and I followed like my life depended on it.

We arrived at his car. It was an older model Honda Civic and it was sky blue. I wasn't a car person so to me it was a Mercedes and anything that had wheels was better than what I had. I glanced inside and to my disappointment it was a manual. *So much for holding his hand on the way home.* He must've seen my face and came to the wrong conclusion as he unlocked and opened the passenger door for me.

"I know, it's not much, but she gets me where I want to go."

I corrected my face and replied, "No, it's not that, it's just...well...ugh, nevermind. It's not that at all. It's great."

He huffed a breath of laughter out of his nose and made sure I was inside before he shut the door behind me. He walked around the hood of the car and I took in his image as he did. He walked with confidence and humility at the same time. He took the time to look quickly at his tires as he carouseled the car. He got in the driver's side and put our bags in the back seat before starting the car up and began to back out. I gave him a very general direction as to how to get to my house and he nodded and began our journey. The car did his bidding dutifully and without complaint. I forced my gaze out of the passenger's window not wanting to stare him down like the stalker that I was. We drove for a few minutes in silence and at the first stop light he stopped the car slowly and then reached out to tug on my hand, but he didn't let go.

"Hey, you awake?" he said trying to provoke me.

"Yeah, I'm just enjoying the ride. I should be asking you how you are still awake."

I can't believe I just said that. What a dork. Somebody needs to tattoo Super Dork on my face.

He nodded and answered, "Nah, I'm good. I wouldn't miss a minute of this." The light changed to green and he growled. "I had to have a stick shift right?" and was forced to let go of my hand.

It wasn't just me who wanted to be touching him. If touching me had even one eighth of the effect on him as it had on me then he felt the warmth, the craving, the need, the consumption. No wonder he was cursing the stick shift. I was, too.

15 minutes later I was guiding him with my pointer finger through Santa Monica to get to my house. He remarked that he came this way often when he wasn't working, headed to the nearby mall and movie theater. He pulled next to the curb by my house and I sat there starting at the house, not wanting to leave him yet. It was as if I was on the border of two different countries and in those countries I was two different people. In one country was my parents, my oppression, my pain, my introverted

self all wrapped up in poverty and worry over the Terrible Twosome and their unrelenting roller coaster of anger.

In my current country I was still introverted, but there was hope. He was my hope and it made me want to emerge from my present self and adhere my being and my life to him; embracing the life he gave me hope that I could have.

He pulled me out of my inflection and said, "Looks like nobody's home. Are you gonna be ok?"

I snorted and said, "Yeah, I'm by myself a lot. It's no big deal, really. But thanks."

He let out a breath with a little too much force and rubbed his buzz cut head crown to forehead.

"When are they coming home?" he asked.

I fidgeted with my jeans... "Um, maybe tomorrow, maybe the next day. Who knows? They went to visit my Aunt in Las Vegas."

He looked angry now and I didn't know where it was directed.

"What's wrong?" I asked.

"Parents just suck sometimes, you know? It's dangerous for a girl to be home alone all the time."

He was wearing the vinyl off of the steering wheel, rubbing it in aggravation and I tried to bring him back down.

"It's ok, really. I've been on my own a lot since I was about twelve or so. I know to lock the doors and I don't go out at night unless I have to work. It's ok. Don't be mad, I'm a big girl." I laughed nervously.

He smiled, too, but it was just to appease me. I understood his anger as it was shared between us but I didn't want to spend my time with him angry at my parents. They stole enough of my joy and my life already.

He put his head on the steering wheel and looked like he was trying to reel in his frustration. "You're right. I just...never mind."

He righted himself in the seat and removed his seat belt.

"Come on, I'll walk you to the door." I reached back and grabbed my bag from the seat and went to open my door but he was there already opening it for me.

"Thanks," I whispered.

We walked the short distance up the corroded driveway up to those crumbling concrete steps. I reached for my keys in the front pocket of my bag and unlocked the door, embarrassed by the force it took to get it open.

I turned to him, "Thanks for bringing me home. Saved me from inhaling bus fumes." I was trying to lighten the mood again, but my jokes were lame.

"It's no problem, J." His new nickname for me did not go unnoticed.

"Anytime I don't work after school I would..."

He rocked back and forth on the heels of his Doc Martens.

"I would be happy to bring you home every day if I could."

I smiled at him and reached out to tentatively touch a button on his shirt. He quietly gasped and I said, "Thank you," again.

He cleared his throat and stepped back two steps.

"Ok, can I still call you tonight?"

"No," I said with the most serious face I could muster.

"You have gone over your Jenna quota for the day. You are dismissed."

He laughed out loud, louder than I've ever heard before, and it was the most glorious sound I had ever heard.

I laughed in return and he said, "You need to up my limits then, because I'm planning on meeting my Jenna quota every day I can."

Leaving me melting on my porch steps he turned and got in his car, started it and then motioned me with a smile and a waving hand to go in the house.

I complied and when I had shut the door he put his car into gear and sped away. I collapsed against the old broken backdoor with the duct tape window and sat there for a half an hour just smiling like my world was complete. I buried my eyes into the palms of my hands and finally admitted to myself the truth. "I love him, even if he doesn't love me. Loving him is enough."

Chapter 8

I went through my routine of work, homework and a Ramen noodle soup dinner. We didn't confirm what time he would call, but I was a ball of nervous, excited energy. I showered and took up temporary residence by the phone. *Yeah, I've progressed passed moron and onto obsessive, sit by the phone and wait moron. Nice.* I lost myself in a new book about a boy who was an Ace trying to find his significant other. I was entranced by it. So much so that when the phone rang I threw the book in the air and then had to "Air Raid" until I made sure it wasn't going to impale me. It plunked on the floor beside me and I picked it up and marked my page with a bookmark. I checked the caller id and it was a local number, the same number as the night before. I took a deep breath and put my hands out in front of my palms down pushing downward trying to move the nervousness away. It didn't work.

"Hello," I said it so cool. I was getting good at this.

"Hey you," he said.

OK, never mind…he was the epitome of cool.

He continued, "What are you doing?"

"Um, I was reading." I really needed to work on not saying 'um'.

He groaned, "I hate reading. When I have to read a book for school I read the beginning and then the end and guess about the rest."

I laughed and answered, "Well, reading is my crack."

He laughed, "Ahhh, well, good to know."

All of the sudden my brave girl surfaced and I started, "Can I ask you a question?"

He chuckled and answered, "Of course, J, ask me anything."

I cleared my throat and asked "When I first came to Drama class and told you that I had been transferred there you said that made things easier for you. What did you mean by that?"

He was quiet way too long and I glanced at the caller id and saw that the call was still active.

"I um....well...I saw you last semester. You were walking between the Administration building and the Commons Area and ever since then I've been trying to find you again. I saw you once through the gate. You were walking towards the bus stop and I walked around the fence but it was too late, you were boarding the bus. So, what I meant was... you being in Drama was easier for me than trying to chase you around all the time."

I replied the only way my throat would let me. "Oh"

There was a long pause...longer than the one that superseded this one.

"Oh, man...I'm scaring you right? I'm telling you too much. I basically just confessed that I'm a stalker."

He let out a violent "whoosh" of breath and it sounded in the phone like someone blowing in a microphone.

"No...it's not that. I just...until just now I thought I was doing a really good job at not being noticed."

He laughed out loud again and it washed over my soul like a cool breeze.

"Well, apparently it didn't work on me."

I laughed, too, and my own free laughter surprised me. We talked about everything and I yawned a little too loudly when it had reached just after 10:00.

"Hey," he said "I'm sorry; we've been on the phone for hours. You probably need to get some sleep."

I laughed. "Me? You, you need to get some sleep."

He chuckled. "Yeah, I kinda do. But I wanted to see if you wanted to go see a movie Friday night."

I answered without thinking. "Yeah, what time?"

He let out a breath and then answered, "How about I just pick you up at 6 and then we can check the movie times and then walk around until it starts?"

"OK, I just have to ask my parents when they get home. But I'm 18 so they can't really say 'No' right?" I laughed, but he didn't.

"Well, ask them when they get back. I'll see you tomorrow, ok? Sleep tight and make sure you lock the doors and everything."

"Yeah, you, too," I hung up the phone and my blissful mood was soured.

My hand was still on the receiver and stayed there while I thought this through. The feeling of doom creeped up my spine like a black virus.

Are they gonna pitch a fit? They don't even speak to me, why would they care? I'm 18, they can't stop me though, right? I've always done everything they asked me to. I make good grades. Why wouldn't they? I have to date sometime right?

All of the sudden I heard a car in the driveway. I sped as quickly as I could to my bedroom, jumped into the bed, and pretended the best I could that I was asleep.

Someone came in and put May to bed and then I heard various bathroom noises and talking and then their bedroom door closed. I slowly let out the breath that I had been holding for what seemed like an hour and let myself relax. I decided that I wouldn't obsess about the what- ifs and focused only on this newfound feeling of wholeness and serenity.

Chapter 9

The next morning was routine. I got up, got dressed in an old French Quarter t shirt and jeans and of course my Chucks. Everyone was asleep and I crept out quietly and got to school.

School was normal school. I forced myself, again, to pay attention just to stop myself from thinking about him every 5 seconds. I walked finally to Drama and there was a note on the theater door that said "End of the Year Party in Classroom".

I turned around and started back the way I came. I entered the classroom last and went directly to a seat in the back corner. As soon as I did Mr. Escobar was clapping his hands in a gesture to gain the class' attention. Everyone stopped talking and faced forward. I let my eyes wander and found the pair of eyes I wished most to see. He was watching the Mr. Escobar as he flailed his hands about as he went on and on about the success of the play and how "wonderful" it was. Carlos was paying attention, but his knee was bouncing, a sign I now recognized as either boredom or nervousness. I leaned my face in my palm and tried not to be so obvious about looking at him. I commanded my eyes to stay on the flamboyant Mr. Escobar as he gushed with praises on our mediocre performances.

He finally finished and I allowed my eyes to wander back to him. Now he was mimicking my posture but looking directly at me almost as a silent plea for me to meet his gaze. He rolled his eyes towards the teacher and it made me smile. Then he started talking to his friends while still peeking at me in perfectly timed intervals. The teacher had brought some Cokes and chips and everyone else was partaking. We were told to spend the rest of the hour as we wanted to. I pulled out a book and kicked back. I was *not* going to go talk to him while he was with his group of guys. Not gonna happen.

I was thoroughly engrossed in the story when a whisp of cinnamon breeze touched me gently on my left side before he sat in the desk next to me.

He turned my book to see the cover and smiled. "You really do love books, huh?"

I blushed. This was it. It was real. He just confirmed what we had talked about on the phone.

I cleared my throat. "Yeah, I read...um...a lot."

He chuckled and ran his hand around my elbow.

"How much is a lot?" he asked.

Why in the heck did he want to know?

"I don't know...about 4 or 5 books a week?"

I was low balling on purpose. I would reveal my true nerd nature at a better time.

"Huh," he said. "So...did you ask your parents about Friday night?"

I got that sinking feeling in my stomach just thinking about talking to them about it. "No, they got home late last night. I will talk to them tonight."

"Oh, well, ok. Maybe you will know by the time I call tonight."

I nodded my head "yes" and then for the rest of the period we talked about movies that we liked. We had different tastes in movies but agreed on the funny ones.

The bell rang too quickly and he said, "Oh hey, I forgot. I've got to take my brother somewhere today, I can't drive you home."

Relief and grief washed over me simultaneously.

"That's ok. It's no big deal. I can ride the bus...always have."

He looked at his shoes and smiled bashfully. "Yeah, but I'd rather it be you in my car. I'll talk to you tonight."

He turned to get his bag and walked away and all I could do was give him a wave, which ended up being a cross between a pageant queen and "jazz hands". I looked at my hand like it wasn't attached and rolled my eyes. *Ugh...*

That night I played my game of "dance by the back door" for a few seconds. I wondered how I was going to bring up the subject of Carlos to my Mom and what she was going to say about it. More importantly, I wondered if I was going to be a coward, or finally stand up for myself. B

Before I could decide, the handle jangled violently and then opened so fast I didn't have time to think.

"It's about time you got home." She spit as she said it and I winced at the sheer volume.

I walked into the house and she slammed the door behind me.

"So..." she said in a fake nice voice "What have you been up to while we were gone?"

I stood there dumbfounded for a second and then she screamed,

"Answer me you stupid little shit!" The small dining room reverberated at the enraged decibels. I stuttered...

"Nothing, I just went to school and did homework and went to work and..."

When she talked to me like this I immediately became a different person. My entire demeanor changed I became 11 years old and scared to the point where I could hardly move, much less answer her questions. The phrase 'scared stiff" was made just for me.

She crept closer to me and my eyes bulged in sync with her steps. She started with a whiny voice, mocking my own...

"And....and...brought a boy over here!"

"No, I didn't," I stammered.

"Oh, so the neighbors lied to us? They just make up random lies to get you in trouble for no reason right? Poor little Jenna. Don't forget little girl that I know every trick you could pull on me because I've pulled it."

My name on her lips was like she was spitting up bile.

"No, I mean, someone dropped me off...but he didn't come in." She clasped her chest and switched to her "nice" voice.

"Oh...and who is this person dropping you off and how are you paying him back? Hmmmmm?"

Tears bobbled on the edges of my bottom eye lids and congregated in the corner of my eyes.

"No," I said as loudly as my little voice could. "He was just being nice. I think...I think he likes me."

The tears broke the invisible dam and flowed in chaotic patterns down my face. I don't know why I confessed that he likes me. It was just asking for it.

She got right in my face and said "Bullshit! Who would ever like you? Huh? I guess that's whose number is on the caller ID, too, huh?"

She began pacing in the living room and I briefly looked to find my May sitting silently on her hands in the living room. She looked like she was on the edge of crying as well. They were making her our audience. And my step-Dad was looking on proudly as my mother berated me as his entertainment. He cleared his throat and began to speak very slowly like he was speaking to a lower life form.

"So you 'think' this boy likes you. What are you gonna do? Hmmm? You think you can just do what you want to now that you're 18? You still live in this house under my roof that I paid for!"

It was then that my mouth betrayed me.

"You can't pay for anything if you don't even work."

Before I could react the back of her hand connected with my cheek bone and hit exactly the spot where it hurt the most. She'd had lots of practice. She was still screaming at me as she dragged me by the arm to my room and locked it behind me. What she said I'll never know. After a minute or so the tears stopped and I got as comfortable as I could for the night. I tried to lie on the opposite side of the stinging to make the blood rush away from the now bruising area.

The whole incident made me think of the time we lived in a complex of run down apartments and I had lost the key to the front door by accident. I had to go to the landlord's apartment and ask her to open the door for me. What I didn't know was that they charged $10 every time they did that for a tenant. The landlord left a note on the door the next day billing us for letting me in. I didn't have money, but that didn't mean I didn't pay for it. I was 8 and it was the first time I can remember being backhanded. My Mom had hit and pushed before but that was the day she first hit me in the face. For some reason hitting people in the face is a lot more personal and heinous than hitting somewhere else or pushing. I later found the key in the bottom of my purse but it was too little too late.

I don't know how much longer it was but soon I was awoken by the phone ringing. Mom answered it and I heard her say, "No, I'm sorry; she doesn't want to talk to you anymore." I could feel the cracking and piercing of shards in my chest as my heart broke. And then she hung up. Her steps then neared the bedroom door, it unlocked with a "click". The light made me blink furiously as I heard her say

"Aww...too bad you can't talk to him. Now get your ass to the shower and then to bed. And you can't go to school looking like that."

She clucked her tongue against the roof of her mouth.

"Too bad...he had a nice voice." She laughed. When she laughed like that she sounded like Cruella DeVille.

I got up and went directly to the bathroom. I looked at myself in the mirror and my eye was puffy underneath and my cheek was purple and grayish looking. I turned on the cold water and took off my clothes and jumped in. The icy water took my breath away but then it felt fantastic on my cheek. I washed my hair and then washed my body with the sliver of soap left for me. I got out and heard them talking in their room. The house was so full of cigarette smoke that I was suddenly glad we didn't own smoke alarms. *Hell, we couldn't even afford a whole bar of soap.* I groaned as I slipped into bed and it was then that everything hit me. And this reality slap was way worse than her backhand could ever be. *She told him that I don't want to talk to him. He must think I'm such a wench. He's never gonna speak to me again.* As I fell asleep my last thought was: *I will still love him...even if I can't have him.*

The next day was spent in silence and necessary whispers. I cleaned the house as thoroughly and silently as possible while they slept. I made them a pot of coffee to avoid the wrath when they woke up. I know the drill. Keep quiet, keep busy and keep complacent. It was how I had survived since my parents divorced and my Mom remarried this tyrant and reformed her discipline methods. Yes, I was somewhat of a coward. But at least I got one good truth into their ears last night. My thoughts drifted to Carlos minute by minute. *He probably noticed that I wasn't in school that day, right? Would he try to call again? How was I going to let him go?* Silent tears snaked rivers down my cheeks as I diligently worked room by room.

They finally got up about noon and announced that they were going somewhere. I took care of May most of the day and called into work feigning sickness. I made May a supper of macaroni and cheese and a can of green beans. They still hadn't returned at 7:30, so I cleaned up the kitchen mess and put the leftovers away and went to bed to read. I wasn't reading more than 10 minutes when the phone rang. I looked over at May quickly to make sure she was asleep.

I bolted out of my bed and looked at the caller ID. It was him. My heart protested against the prison of my sternum and wanted to jailbreak. I picked up the receiver so quickly that I had to play a little game of "hot potato" with it to steady my hands.

Finally I got it to my ear and said, "Hello?"

Carlos gasped on the other side of the phone. "Jenna...Thank God...Are you ok?"

All my anxiety left my body at the sound of his voice.

"Yeah, I'm..uh...ok... now."

"What the hell happened?" he yelled.

I thought he was angry, so I went into a rambling of apologies.

"I'm so sorry. My Mom found out that you brought me home and she accused me of some weird stuff and then she...um...I couldn't talk on the phone. I know you're angry. I DID want to talk to you."

I was still on my rant when he said, "Hey, hey, stop...I'm not mad. Shit...I've been worried sick. If you didn't answer the phone I was 2 minutes from coming over there and knocking until someone answered. I figured something was wrong when your Mom told me that last night but then you didn't come to school...I mean I had a bad feeling about your parents..."

He went silent like he was remembering the day.

"I'm sorry. I couldn't come to school today. You'll probably see why tomorrow."

He didn't say anything for a while and I said, "You there?"

He let out a breath that he was apparently holding and said, "Yeah, I'm here. Just so we're clear...what am I gonna see tomorrow?"

I stalled, "It's not a big deal...I just couldn't come today."

I could hear a tapping sound and imagined the noise was his foot on the floor as his knee bobbed up and down.

"Jenna...you have no idea...thinking about why you wouldn't talk to me yesterday and then you didn't show up today...I mean you don't worry about someone that much unless..."

Every muscle in my body had tensed at hearing his words.

"Unless what?" I whispered. Now he was whispering.

"Unless it's someone you love."

My defenses suddenly went up like metal walls in an FBI building.

"Don't joke about that."

He was silent for a few seconds too long and then he said "Jenna...I'm not joking. I know it's fast, but I think I've... well since the moment I saw you through that gate. It seems like I was just biding my time until you."

Car lights came through the windows like warning signs reflected in the dirty glass.

"Hey, I think they're home. I gotta go. And, Carlos?" I said it really, really fast.

"Yeah," he said.

I could hear a sound like he stood up and his chair legs pushed back against the floor. My rabbit heart fluttered in building the courage.

"I love you more."

I hung up the phone quickly and pressed the "erase" button on the caller ID. I then ran on my tip toes to my room and flounced into my bed. I forced my breathing to mimic sleep as my insides still shook from his revelation. I listened to the normal sounds of "them" as they tromped through the house noisily and then went to bed. *He loved me. This guy who is sweet and kind and gorgeous, he loves...me. No, no matter what... I'm not giving him up.*

Chapter 10

The next morning I tried to cover what was left of the already yellowing bruise on my cheek with concealer. I also wore my hair braided to the side of my face so that some of my not curly, but not straight wisps fall on that side of my face. I walked through school and remained unnoticed by most. The famous last period came around and when I entered the classroom the chairs were back in a circle formation. "Crap" I muttered under my breath. We only had about six weeks left of school. Was he seriously going to make us do another play?

Mr. Escobar came in and laughed so loud that I ducked my head in response. He pointed his trigger finger at everyone and imaginary shot them one by one and said "Gotcha" I rolled my eyes. He told us that for the rest of the semester we could use the period as a study hall.

I made my way to the corner acting like I didn't know who was already there waiting for me. I looked up in false horror.

"Hey, you're in my seat," I said. *When did I get so cheeky and brave?*

He laughed that soul soothing laugh and moved to the next seat.

"I was warming it up for you." I smiled at him and laughed back.

He turned his chair so that it was face to face with my desk and touching each other. He raised his hand in the air slowly, pulled back and started again. He touched my face with the backs of his fingers so gently I barely even felt it. Then he turned his hand to touch my bruise with the pads of his fingers. They were rough and calloused but felt like heaven, warm heaven.

"Is this why you couldn't come to school?"

I nodded and he put his hands on the desk and clenched and unclenched them repeatedly. His knee was jerking furiously again.

I let out a breathy, "Stop; it's ok."

He shook his head "no" and started up again. I tentatively reached out and covered his hands with as much of my tiny hands as I could.

He instantly let up and said, "I wanna talk about this later."

I nodded and we sat silently for a few minutes. He pulled out a notebook and pencil and began to draw. He had it tilted towards him so I couldn't see and I squinted my eyes at him in aggravation. He was drawing something. He just smiled and kept working. My angry face wasn't very intimidating apparently.

Minutes ticked by and then he handed me a note on a piece of paper that read:

Are we going out tonight or not?

I scribbled back:

Yes.

He stared at it a minute and then wrote:

What about your parents?

I groaned out loud and he chuckled and I took the pencil back from him and wrote:

I'm gonna talk to them today when I get home. Anyway, are you off work today?

He responded quickly.

Yeah. I asked for the day off. I have to take my brother to work tonight though. I'm gonna work short shifts on Saturday and Sunday during the day instead. Then I go back Monday night. Pick you up at 6:00?

I remembered I had to work that night and I wrote:

I have to work until 6:30. Can you pick me up at 7:30? I need to shower and change.

He blushed as he read this and it was the sexiest thing I had ever seen in my life. I wanted to climb over the desk and bite his lower lip. But I couldn't imagine what he was blushing at. I gave him a questioning look with my eyebrows slightly furrowing. He started drawing a line on the paper and then showed it to me. **Shower** was underlined. I quickly wrote back:

Gutter brain

I hid my face with my hands and he laughed nervously as he wrote back to me.

Ok, I will see you at 7:30. Parents?

I rolled my eyes and went to reply, but the bell rang.

We moved our desks back in place and I turned back to talk to him.

I looked him dead in the eyes and I said, "I'm eighteen years old and I've only ever gone out with groups of people. I won't let them stop me."

He put both hands on each side of my waist and gave a slow squeeze.

He matched my direct eye contact and said, "Don't let them stop you...please."

He started walking toward the door and glanced back one last time to smile at me. I left shortly after I could move my legs again.

I rode the bus home and took that time to gather my courage in order to face what I had to tonight. I got home and directly went into my parents' room to say what I had to say. I walked into the room and started in without even saying "hello". I made my voice stay solid and firm.

"So," I began. "Carlos is the boy who brought me home the other day and that's him who was calling while you were gone..." I waved my hand in the air ... "Wherever. I'm 18 and I work and put in for groceries here. He asked me to go to the movies tonight and I'm going. First I'm going to work and then he's picking me up at 7:30. I'm simply telling you so that you'll know."

Man, I'm gonna get my butt beat for that one. I raised my eyebrows and crossed my arms over my chest in satisfaction that I had gotten all I needed to say out. Even if they were the last words I would ever mutter.

My Mom and the Tyrant smirked at each other and he said "Fine. But your date..." He sneered the word "date". "Is going to have to come in and let us meet him first." I shrugged one shoulder and noticed that my Mom was in pure shock at the conversation being held in front of her. Her eyes were bulged at my Step-Dad trying to convey a secret message to him.

"Ok, that's fine," I said all smug with myself.

I didn't give them an opportunity to say anything else. Instead I got dressed and picked on May for playing for playing with Pet Shops and then went to work early to try to make up my hours. Before I left I scrolled through the caller id and wrote down Carlos' number. As soon as I got out of view of the house on my way to the music store I had to stop and lean against the concrete of the freeway underpass. I let out a long breath that I could swear I had been holding for hours. I then started giggling to myself. It was there perched against a crumbling concrete column under the freeway that my hope, the hope I saw in my new found love, turned from a feeling into truth.

I started to do my regular duties at work in a hurry. There was a method to my madness today. I vacuumed and dusted the whole store and straightened the shelves that needed it. I finally made my way behind the desk and retrieved the sheet music that needed to be filed because it was in the wrong place, returned or the customer changed their mind. I brought it to the storeroom which was hidden in this cool door which was flush against the wall and if you didn't know there was a door there you wouldn't be able to tell. I hurried in and closed the door behind me and first sorted the sheet music alphabetically by composer. I snuck a look out through a small window on the side to ensure that no one was coming and took my chance. I called the number I found on the caller id and shuffled back and forth on my feet as it rang.

I nearly knocked over the shelves beside me when I heard the voice my heart desired answer, "Hello?" His voice literally melted me.

I giggled a little, "Hi! It's Jenna."

I could hear the smile in his voice when he answered, "Hey!! You called. Aren't you at work?"

I sighed. "Yeah, I took a…um…break to call you and let you know that we're still on for tonight."

He breathed into the phone. "Good, I was kinda worried after the last couple of days that they weren't gonna let you go."

I smiled. "Well, I gotta get off of this phone before I get caught. I can't talk long. But I wanted to let you know that I can go."

He sighed. "Ok, I'll see you at seven thirty. Bye."

I purposely didn't tell him that he had to meet my parents. He hung up first this time and I was glad. It was hard to hang up on him. I filed all of the music with a spring in my step and before I knew it six thirty had rolled around.

I ran home and showered and got dressed ignoring the snide remarks and mean comments my Mom was giving me. I looked in my closet and instantly panicked. *I have nothing to wear.* I pulled out a decent pair of jeans and found a cute black shirt which had some kind of design in white down one side. I wore my cheap black Mary Jane's and headed to the bathroom to make myself look less like "death warmed over". My bruises were barely visible now. She must not have been as strong or as good of aim as she thought. I put on some minimal makeup and remembered that I had a pair of black flower earrings in my top drawer. I put them on and put on some scented lotion that I had bought with one of my paycheck leftovers. I walked out of my room and ran right into my Mom.

I gathered some gall and said, "Well, do I look ok?"

She glared at me and said, "As good as *you* can get, I guess."

She went to sit on the couch next to my Step-Dad and they just sat there while I cleaned up the bathroom and kept myself busy getting ready.

The doorbell rang at 7:25 and I smiled at his early arrival. I headed towards the door to open it but was intercepted by my step Dad.

"Good try." He smiled a creepy smile at me.

I shuddered and goose bumps, not the good ones, came to life on my arms.

He opened the door and shook Carlos' hand and invited him in. Carlos smiled at me and I tried to give him a look that conveyed "I'm sorry".

He walked up to my Mom, who was seething on the couch, and said, "Nice to meet you. I'm Carlos."

She gave him the most horrible smile and then said "Yeah, have her home on time or else it won't be nice to meet me."

I palm slapped my forehead and said "Um...yeah...let's go or we'll be late for the movie."

Carlos caught my drift and nodded, "Yeah, we're about to miss it."

"She needs to be home by eleven and if she's not, don't think about taking her out again." I rolled my eyes not only at her tone, but at her all-the-sudden need to be my mother.

We made our way out to his car and he opened the door for me. I slipped in, reached over, and unlocked the driver's side door for him.

"Thanks," he said as he slid into the driver's seat and started the car.

"The movie doesn't start until 8:30, but I thought we could walk around the Promenade until then."

I shrugged, not really caring where we went as long as I was with him.

"Yeah, that's fine."

We made our way to the Promenade. It was a Friday night so it was alive with music and street performers and people of every color, shape and size. There were twinkly lights strung everywhere and the smells of fried fair food permeated the air.

As soon as we parked, he walked to my side and took my hand and said "By the way, I didn't get a chance to tell you how great you look tonight."

I bumped my shoulder with his and said, "Thanks, you look pretty good yourself."

He smiled and said, "Let's go get our tickets so we don't have to worry about it."

I nodded, "Yeah, that's fine."

Our hands almost immediately found each other fit together as though they were made one for the other. He bought our tickets after a small amount of protest from me for not getting to pay for my own. We walked through some shops around the movie theater, just browsing and waiting for the movie to start.

We talked about nothing and everything and there was a calmness around my soul that I didn't think I had ever felt in my life. I was at peace. It was if I could finally breathe. We laughed and he huffed and puffed when I told him about my Mom slapping me the other night. I shrugged it off and tried to tell him that it wasn't something that happened every day and that hopefully I would be leaving soon, either for college or just to get out. We talked about his plans after school and then the movie started. We were "shhhhed" by some older people in front of us. It made us laugh and when they did it again we laughed even harder.

The movie started and the lights went low and suddenly I was nervous. I mean, I had barely kissed one or two guys before and they were sloppy, messy, icky experiences that I had tried to forget. Was he going to kiss me? He must've sensed my change in mood because he turned and gave me a questioning glance. Suddenly I wasn't nervous anymore. He moved the arm rest from being in between us to between the tops of our seats. Now it was my turn to look at him questioningly. He looked forward to the movie screen and huffed out this big breath and then looked back to me swiftly and put his arm around my shoulders and gently nudged my shoulder with his hand gesturing me to move closer. I moved a little towards him not knowing how close to get.

His smooth voice was suddenly in my ear, "Come on, J, it's just me."

I bit my lip and reveled in the new feelings he was bringing forward in me. I scooted, gathering my bravery, all the way over to him and shimmied until I was comfortable in the crook of his arm. He chuckled and kissed my temple and whispered "Much better."

The movie ended and it was supposed to be some kind of action movie but other than the commercial I had seen briefly on TV, I had no idea what it was about. We stayed put until the theater had emptied. I looked at him warily and asked the time. He said it was only 10:00, so we had an hour to find something to do. We walked the short distance to a small park with lots of benches. We were technically still on the promenade but in a secluded area. The park overlooked the ocean, but it was still a good distance away. I put my hands on the almost rotted away wooden gate. You'd think that a fence which separated the people from falling over a cliff to the ocean would be stronger and sturdier. The sun had mostly gone down and its remnants lingered on top of the waves.

We stayed there silent for a while absorbing the peace.

He cleared his throat. "So, are we gonna talk about what you said to me on the phone the other night?"

I knew exactly what he was getting at, but I played like I didn't.

I smiled and said, "What? I really like to read...so what."

He laughed a haughty genuine laugh and said looked at me fiercely.

"That's not really what I was talking about and you know it."

I put a smug grin on my face and replied, "Well, at least I said it and didn't just hint around it."

He backed up looking shocked and said, "What? I said it."

I quickly responded, "No you didn't. You said you worried about me and that you don't worry about people like that unless you love them. That's sooo not saying it."

I raised one eyebrow at him and he laughed again.

"Well, you definitely said it. I heard you."

I sighed heavily and looked back at the ocean.

"Yeah, I did. Too bad you're not gonna hear it again until I hear it from you first."

So...I thought that was going to prompt him to say it but he didn't.

I suddenly realized that a good amount of time had lapsed. My eyes grew wide as I nearly screamed "What time is it?"

He looked at his watch and said, "Crap, it's 10:40!"

My face gave my emotions away. I was freaking out. "It's ok. We'll make it."

We started to walk/run towards the parking garage. I was so completely consumed by worry about the repercussions of being late that I didn't even enjoy the ride home. I twisted my hands in worry and he kept looking at me with concern written all over his face.

"Jenna, we're gonna get there on time."

I nodded, that's all I could muster then conjured, "I know, just hurry please."

He pulled curbside my house at 10:57 and as soon as we pulled up the lights on the small porch lit up like she was waiting for us. I looked at him regretting that this was the way our first date was to end.

He looked up at the house and said "I'm sorry, J. I'm really sorry. Next time I will watch the clock closer. I hate to think..."

I put my hand on the handle; the time was now 10:59.

I grabbed his right hand with my left and intertwined our fingers for a few seconds.

"I know, it's ok. See you later."

There was no time for him to even think about anything other than saying "goodbye" and I was out of his car and into my backdoor. I looked at the kitchen clock and it read 11:00 sharp. My Mom was standing in the doorway between the kitchen and the dining room with her hands on her hips. She said nothing but gave me a smirk and went to her bedroom. In my relief I nearly doubled over the rusty stove and hugged it. I reveled momentarily in the cool metal of the burners against my flaming cheeks. I went to my room and changed into an old t shirt and my comfiest pajama pants. I brushed my teeth and washed my face and went back to the bedroom. May was already asleep. She had some chocolate on the corner of her little lips and I wiped it off. They didn't make her brush her teeth before bed. Oh well, at least she got fed. I pulled back my covers and slipped into bed. I turned on my side towards the window and hugged myself around the middle trying to keep those once felt feelings of serenity lull me to sleep.

Six a.m. on a Saturday pisses me off to no end. I had to be to work for seven a.m. and I was starving. Not hungry, but starving. I checked my wallet in my messenger bag and looked to see if I had any cash. *Wait! I have 10 bucks stashed in case I had to buy my ticket last night! Score!* I had tucked the rest of my paycheck into my dresser drawer and swore to myself that I wouldn't touch it.

I rushed to take a quick shower and twirled my hair up into a messy bun and headed out. I went to a small Swedish bakery three doors down from the music store and headed in. They made the most glorious cream cheese filled croissants ...ever. I ordered one with a medium cappuccino and sat down to my little piece of divinity.

With two minutes left until my shift started I walked towards the store. I was entranced and bothered by Carlos' and my date last night. There were no first kisses goodnight and no romantic goodbyes. There was me acting like a spaz trying to get out of his car as fast as I could to avoid my Mom's wrath. I'm such a fraidy cat. I could kick myself for being so scared. But on the other side if I didn't get home on time I wouldn't be allowed to see him for a long time, maybe ever again. I chose at that moment to bury my thoughts not in what was but what did happen. He smiled at me, he held me and we had laughed together. He worried about me. More importantly I loved him and I would see him again.

Sunday came and went and I was more eager than ever to welcome Monday. I was glad that he hadn't attempted to call on Sunday and I remembered that he was working to make up for missing Friday night.

I was walking to my homeroom class, in my own bubble. I went to my locker to get rid of some of my book weight and at first I thought my eyes were deceiving me.

Carlos was there, back leaned against my locker, feet crossed at the ankles and his arms were crossed over his chest. His head was leaned back against the locker and his eyes were closed. He managed to be cool and hot as hell at the same time. I snuck up on him and poked him in the ribs.

He jumped, wide eyed and I said, "Hey, no sleeping on my locker."

He laughed and lunged at me hugging me around my shoulders like he hadn't seen me in months. He rubbed his cheek against the side of my head and I tucked my face into the side of his neck. It was like breathing in an entire Aspen forest. It was the best feeling ever.

"I may or may not have begged Mrs. Alma to tell me where your locker was."

"That Mrs. Alma, I'm gonna have to report her," I said.

He laughed, "Yeah, well, it was worth it."

"Why? So you could get a nap in?" I joked.

"Yeah, do you mind?" He laughed and resumed his leaned back napping.

I was not backing down.

"Nope, not at all. Don't let me bother you."

I took off as fast as my stubby legs could take me down the hall and as my foot touched down on the first stair I felt strong buffed out arms grab me around my middle and pull me back to the second floor.

"Ok, Ok, you win. I found your locker so I could see you first thing in the morning instead of waiting all freakin' day until 6th period." He laughed.

"Awww..." I cooed at him.

"Come on, didn't you need to get into your locker."

"Not really, I was just told there was a hot guy there. I guess he left." I cocked my eyebrow at him.

"Ouch," he said jokingly.

We walked back to my locker and I put half of my books back in it from the weekend.

"Where's your homeroom?"

" The Science Building. You?" I asked.

"Ugh, all the way out by the Driver's Ed. Class." He groaned.

He was right. It was a long hot walk all the way out there. The warning bell startled us both a little.

"So..." I started, "I guess I'll see you in sixth."

He did this thing where he poked his bottom lip out and looked like he was thinking. It made me wonder what his lips felt like. He caught me looking at his lips and smiled.

"We'll see if I can make it sooner. I bet I can."

"How?" I asked.

"I have my ways."

And with that he walked down the hall, the same way I had walked before and before he stepped onto the stairs he waved. I was too busy dreaming up creative ways we could meet up during the day to wave back.

Chapter 11

Every time I left one class and made my way to another I looked out for him. After third period, making my way to fourth period, I gave up. It was already half way through the day and I hadn't spotted him even once. This was my first mistake, letting my guard down. My second mistake was giving up on him.

I came into the Language Arts building and needed to make my way up the stairs to AP Civics. I turned with the herd making my way towards the stairs when my eyes found him down the hall. I wanted to see him, but I also didn't want him to win. He had a look on his face like a jaguar which had zeroed in on his prey. My heart jolted and I did what any worthy prey would do…I ran… up the stairs at a furious pace taking out half of the other students in the process. I squeezed and moved my shoulders in unnatural angles trying to outwit my hunter.

When I got to the top of the stairs I leaned out over the railing at the top and saw his face smiling back up at me. I wiggled my eyebrows at him smugly and he shook his head at me and walked out but not before he was nearly trampled by the now tardy herd.

I waited for fourth period to end and before I even tried to make it out to the Science Building I looked out of the window for the other player in our two player game. I didn't see him anywhere. So I walked back down the stairs and intended to scurry across the Quad to the Science building. I slowed my walk as I got closer, confident that he wouldn't find me now. I walked into the building and into my classroom and sat, proud as a peacock, knowing I had outsmarted him again.

Class began and about 5 minutes into it, the phone on the wall began to ring. Mrs. Credence answered it, opening her lab jacket and sticking his fist on her hip with a huff. She 'mmmhhhmmed' and "unnnhunnned" for a few seconds and then turned with the phone still to her ear.

She looked directly at me, annoyed, and said "Jenna, you're needed to the computer lab for some type of project."

I looked around wide-eyed. I had never been called out of class, plus, I didn't have computer lab or a project.

I gathered my things and put my bag across my chest and headed to the computer lab. It was right down the hall and I hesitantly poked my head into the door. There was only one student and one teacher. I put my hands on my hips and smiled.

"Where's the project?" I said.

The big bellied teacher smiled and laughed a jolly laugh and pointed to the student. Then he went into an office which connected to the lab.

"There's an extremely important project right over there," he said as he exited.

Carlos turned around in the computer chair and smiled the smirk of a person who had just won a round of "hide and seek".

I squinted my eyes and gave him my most angry look, which wasn't very intimidating and asked, "You think you're funny?"

He laughed and said, "No, I think I am ingenius."

I relented and sat down in the chair next to him, sighed and said, "True."

I looked around and said, "Where are all the other students?"

He looked around as well and said "Oh, this is the one period where there is no computer lab. And I have Independent Study this hour, so Mr. Rhodes usually lets me hang out in here."

I let out a small huff of breath and smiled, "Good to know."

We talked and joked around for the rest of the hour and both groaned when the bell rang for the next class.

"See you later," he said as we began to walk in separate directions after leaving the building.

Sixth period finally arrived and I spent most of it reading...well, pretending to read. Carlos spent a few minutes talking to his friends. He was sitting on the very edge of the chair and doing that knee bobbing thing and he kept looking back and forth between me and his friends. I couldn't help but giggle, but tried to cover my mouth to cover it up.

He got up, and walked to my corner of the classroom and I glued my eyes to the book in front of me pretending not to see him. He moved the desk beside me to in front of me and just sat there. After reading the paragraph at the top of the page about three times over, I looked up at him.

"Is it funny?" he asked with the greatest grin on his face.

"Is what funny?" I really didn't know what he was referring to.

"Your book. You've been trying to hide your giggling over here for about ten minutes." *How did he see I was giggling?*

"Um..no...not really. I was laughing about something else."

"Oh, really, now I'm curious. What is it?" He rested his chin in his palm and waited for his answer. *Like he doesn't know.*

"If you must know..." He raised his eyebrows so he must need to know. "I was laughing at you over there perched on the edge of your chair, and you were doing that thing with your knee. You weren't even paying attention to your friends, you were just nodding. It was funny." I dipped my chin slightly, satisfied that I'd gotten all of that out.

He got this immensely serious look on his face and said "So...you were watching me?" One of his eyebrows went up a little as he finished his question.

I scrunched my face up in embarrassment and looked up at the ceiling. He grabbed my hands and rubbed his thumbs and fingertips over my fingertips.

"J, look at me," he said and he was whispering and it made me shiver all over.

I slowly met his gaze and blew out a breath. I was caught. And it humiliated that hell out of me. I was so new at this... And so bad at this.

"You have no poker face, you know that?" He continued to whisper.

"I really don't. I blush at everything. Sorry." I felt like my chest cavity was wide open. Not only had I let down my walls, but they were down and crushed on the ground and I was open and it was completely new and weird and uncomfortable and freeing.

"It's a really great blush." His voice was gentle and I knew he was sincere.

"I..." I tried to croak out a 'Thank you' but there was no use. That bell had a personal vendetta against me.

He said quickly, "So...can I take you home again?"

My eyes went wide and my heart trampolined down to my stomach and up into my throat at the thought of the chastising I would endure if they were home when I got home.

"Hey," he said... "It's ok, I was just hoping..."

"No!" He instantly misunderstood. "I mean, no, I'm not going to let them scare me out of everything. I would really like a ride home."

He rubbed the top of his short black hair and was thinking about it. It was a sight to behold and I flexed my hands behind my back protesting their need to feel it for myself.

"Ok, if you're sure." He finally grinned, but it wasn't a full-on smile.

"We'd better hurry up. You are getting close to your Jenna quota."

He laughed and we walked out of the classroom, then the building. We got into his car and took off towards my house.

"Are you hungry or anything?" He looked over at me. There's this feeling you get when someone asks you if you want food or something to drink but they are really asking because *they* are hungry or thirsty.

"Not really. I mean I could use a Coke. Are you?" I sang the 'you' part to let him know I was onto him.

"Yeah..." he laughed... "I'm starving. But I can wait."

"No, it's fine. Anyway, I usually get home a lot later. So it's not a big deal."

"Ok, where?" he asked as he drove that stubborn stick shift.

" I don't care. Anywhere." *And I would. I would go anywhere with him.*

We drove around for a while and then we stopped at this taco stand that had the most divine carne asada tacos ever. I had never had them and got this flabbergasted "What? You've never had..." he sighed and shook his head. We ate and talked and talked some more. About 20 minutes before I usually arrived home, we left.

We pulled up at the blue house with the unkempt yard and I was so relieved that they weren't home that my whole body allowed itself to relax. It was as if I was in a full body cast and someone had just cut it off.

He asked me if we could go out again this Saturday, during the day.

I said, "of course."

We decided that he would pick me up at three so that he could go home after work and get some rest and my shift at the music store ended at two.

I tried not to stay in the car too long because I didn't want to get caught by my parents or tattle tailed on by my nosey neighbors either. But truth be told, if he had suggested driving away and never looking back...if it wasn't for May...I would've gone in a heartbeat.

I threaded my small childlike fingers through his warm calloused ones and sighed all the things I was feeling.

He shook my hand to wake me from my pity party and said, "I don't want you to go but I don't want you to stay here and get in trouble either. You know?"

All I could do was nod.

I reached up out of pure instinct and ran my hands down the back of his skull trimmed hair. He looked at me in a way I had never been looked at before and couldn't explain.

Then the loudest horn I had ever heard blared from behind us. We both turned around and there was a huge truck trying to get around Carlos' car to get onto the freeway. We said a quick, "See you tomorrow." The horn blared again as I scrambled to get out of the car so he could drive out of the way of the trucker with the Jeeper's Creepers horn attached to his truck.

I walked up the drive feeling a loss of something. I felt the loss of his presence and was reminded of my life as I turned the knob to that horrible white door with the sad duct taped window.

Chapter 13

That afternoon and night went as close to normal as I get. I went to work, and when I got home my mom and step-dad were home so I finished some homework and played with May. She had gotten a toy as a treat for good work in her new preschool. Who knows where they got the money for that, or *if* they bought it.

School was now a joy for me. Not because I was escaping my life or trying to distract myself from my disturbed parents, but because I had something to look forward to. And there was someone there who cared. There was someone there who apparently looked for my arrival and searched for me in the halls the way I did for him.

He had made an appearance at my locker every morning since and I could almost tell you down to the second when I would see him in between classes. But I couldn't help but have a knot in my gut. It was all going too well, too fast and my parents were way too complacent about my going out. It was a feeling of impending doom, waiting for the other shoe to drop.

We decided during Drama class that we were going to go to the Santa Monica pier. I had only been a few times and when I had we didn't have any money for rides or games or anything. I left that out of the conversation.

Carlos had to go to work that night so I rode the bus home and everyone was home when I got home. May was playing outside in the yard, which was typical. She waved at me and showed me her soup she was making which was actually dirty water in a pail with leaves. I went to work and got another paycheck. I still had not spent mine from the last payday, so I decided to go to the thrift store to look for something new to wear on Saturday.

The lady at the Barely Worn thrift store was a younger woman, maybe 26 or 27 and I could never remember her name but she remembered mine every time. She reminded me of the record store owner on the movie Pretty in Pink...The one who wore clothes that made her look like a different character every day.

Today she had on this black leather jacket with the sleeves rolled up and she had dyed her short hair black. She had tons of black eyeliner on...I took a guess.

"Joan Jett?"

She laughed and said, "Yeah Jenna, 80's Joan Jett. Good guess."

"Thanks."

I looked around a bit. There was absolutely no order to the store whatsoever. It was total chaos. You could never tell if the pants you found had been there for years and you had overlooked them or if they were a new item. And Joan Jett wasn't going to tell you either.

I found a really cute navy blue scoop neck shirt that cinched on the sides with a gray ribbon. I also bought two pairs of jeans, a new sweater and a pair of lavender Chucks. Because you could never have enough Chucks. I also found May a new set of pajamas with little bottles of fingernail polish on them. I paid Joan and decided to get home and wash my 'new' clothes so I could wear them on Saturday.

I stopped by the used bookstore and traded books for my store credit for selling my read books back to her. Happy with my purchases, I headed home to finish my homework for the weekend so I wasn't stuck doing it on Friday.

I got home and my Mom and Step-Dad were waiting in the kitchen hopping up and down on their toes. The nutcracker dancers had nothing on these two.

My Mom sneered at my bags and said, "Oh, excuse us Ma'am, little shopping diva, but we need to go…somewhere. Could you come down off of your high horse for a little while and watch May?"

"Mom, I spent twelve dollars. My books were free because I had store credit."

"Well, whatever, it must be nice."

"Yeah, I'm happy to watch May. Has she eaten dinner?"

Rage ignited her face and she grabbed me by the throat and got so close into my face that I could see the red lines in the whites of her eyes.

"Look you snotty bitch, we fed her ok? Ugh..we're late now. Thanks."

She let go of my throat and I stumbled back a bit into the refrigerator.

My Step-Dad laughed and said, "Don't fall." He shoved past me and they started the car and flew out of the driveway.

I put my own hand around my throat where she had and brought back my hand to look. There was a little blood. I made my way to the bathroom after throwing my bags onto my bed and went into the bathroom to inspect the damage. It wasn't bad, there were just some scratches under my jawline and one was a little deeper than the other and was seeping a tiny amount of blood. It cleaned up with warm water and I went to find May.

I found May playing in her usual spot in the backyard, by herself and her blonde curls were tipped with mud and she was concentrating so hard that she had her little pink tongue out while she worked. She had little purple overalls on with a white t shirt underneath that looked a little too snug around the tops of her arms.

"Hey..." I sat down cross-legged beside her. "What's for dinner tonight?"

She caught on to my game at once.

"Well, Madam, tonight we're having salad with chowder."

I gave her an incredulous look.

"Really? Chowder? Have you ever eaten chowder?"

She stopped stirring and her tongue took a trip to her top lip to help her think.

"No, but there's a guy named Chowder on t.v. and they said it was like soup."

"It is..." I giggled at her "You're right. Did you eat dinner?"

She gave me the hardest meanest glare that her four year old face could muster, put her hand on her hip and huffed.

"Do you call a Pop-Tart dinner?"

"No Ma'am...I call it a Pop-Tart."

She laughed and said, "I call it gross. They asked if I wanted soup and I said 'no' even though I did."

We laughed for a while and she showed me how to make a perfect leaf chowder garnished with bark.

"Hey Sprite...I think *someone* got you some new pajamas today."

She dropped everything and said, "I wanna see. I wanna see!"

We went inside and we made chicken soup because she was apparently on a soup kick inside and outside. She took a bath and after she was dried we did a very extravagant 'new pajama' reveal.

She put her new pajamas on and hopped into bed. I thought about sneaking to call Carlos but I remembered that he was at work. He worked from 7 p.m. until 2 a.m. that night. I took my own shower and got into bed pretty early. I started on one of my newish books and took solace in the peace and quiet.

When the car lights flooded my window I looked at my alarm clock and it was 3:14 am. What in the world could unemployed people be doing out until 3 o'clock in the morning? Maybe it was better if I didn't know. It might make me an accomplice.

I went to work the next morning. It was really busy in the store and there were tons of different types of sheet music to re-shelve. The Los Angeles Symphony Orchestra had been in during the week and had plowed trough every piece that we had.

I got off at 1:30. I was supposed to leave at noon but I hadn't finished re-shelving all of the music so I stayed to finish...not to mention the overtime.

I rushed home and got into the shower. My parents and May were gone so I could be giddy for my date in relative peace. I put on my newish outfit and decided on some flip flops instead of the Chucks. I went to grab some of the cash leftover from my last paycheck. I opened the dresser and rooted around in my usual spot under the old wooden box that I used for my jewelry but came up empty. I thought I must've put it in my purse so I checked there. Nothing. Then it hit me.

Now wonder they had hit the town in such a hurry. That's why they were waiting for me to get home. They had hit a small jackpot. They were doing whatever they do on my dime. They've stooped to stealing from their daughter. Well, I was my mom's daughter, not his. That fact had been pointed out to me on more than one occasion. I blew out an exasperated breath and grabbed twenty dollars from my latest paycheck. I decided I wasn't even going to say anything to them about it. It just wasn't worth it. Either they were going to deny it, claim it was theirs for living there, or I was going to pay with my face. Just not worth it.

Carlos pulled up to the curb a few minutes before three and I was waiting outside for him. I was sitting on the steps outside that faithful white door. I just couldn't sit in that house anymore. My chin was between my knees and I was studying the driveway like it was giving me a grade. I heard his car pull up and his tires crunch against the curb, but I couldn't bear to look at him yet.

He got out of the car and sat on the front of the car on the corner closest to the house. He crossed his ankles and firmly folded his arms over his chest. He had a smug smile plastered to those luscious full lips.

"Um...J?" he re-crossed his legs in the other direction, "I would've come to the door to get you."

He had that exasperated look again like I was a child covered in chocolate that he didn't know how to control but you couldn't help but smile at.

I looked up and his image was blurry from the bubble of tears that hung on for dear life to the edges of the cliff that were my bottom eyelids. I always tried my damndest not to cry, but I felt like it was safe to cry with him around.

I blinked to readjust my vision and the tears bobbled and weaved down my face. It was a loss of control that I hated.

He immediately got off of the hood of the car, put his keys in his pocket and came towards me. He squatted in front of me and put his arms around my calves and placed his chin gently where mine just left.

"Jenna, tell me what happened," he whispered. Peppermint again.

"I will, I just...Can we get away from here first?" I stammered out.

"Yeah." He squeezed my calves. "Let's go."

He helped me to stand up and when we walked to the car he was a little bit behind me and had his left arm all the way around my waist and his hand was splayed on my stomach. It was as if he was holding me up without invading my space. It was the most tender touch I had ever felt. It was as if his touch had belonged to me all along.

He opened the door for me and as we drove away from the house, so the hurt and stress was driven from my body.

We arrived at the Santa Monica Pier and we parked in the parking lot to the left of the Pier. It was hot enough outside, but the surfers and swimmers still had wetsuits on, so the ocean must not have caught up yet.

We stopped and I stared out of the windshield not ready to let go of the explanation for my tears. And he let me. He held my hand and let me be. As if by instinct he knew exactly what I needed, he let me stare and breathe in and out without questions or expectations.

After a few minutes, I turned to him and cleared my throat, "I'm sorry."

He raised his eyebrows and answered, "You're apologizing for crying?"

I laughed at my own pitiful words. I shrugged, "Sorry."

He turned his bottom lip out again. A telltale sign I now recognized. Something snarky was about to exit that beautiful mouth.

"So..." he began as he tried desperately not to smile, "Now you're sorry for being sorry that you cried?"

We both busted out laughing at that one.

Our laughter died down finally, but his bandage had been applied well.

He cleared his throat and said, "Spit it out."

I looked at him sideways and lost all of my resolve to keep my walls up.

I sighed before I rattled off, "I saved my last paycheck. Well, most of it, to use in case of an emergency and I went to get some of it for tonight and it was gone. They took it. I wondered why they were in such a hurry to get out of the house last night and that's why. They found my money and they took it and spent it God knows where on God knows what. Now if May or I need something there is no money, none. I mean I'm really not shocked that they took it, but I feel better when I have something put away."

I took a deep breath. It was all out there. My humility was peaked and I waited to see what he would think.

"They *stole* your paycheck money?" he was truly alarmed.

"Yeah, I had it in my dresser under my jewelry box. I try to change hiding spots every two weeks. And I went to get it and it was gone. It's not the first time," I explained.

He sucked in a very deep breath, aligned his lips together in a straight line and closed his eyes. It was like one of those anger management therapies where they tell you to close your eyes and count to ten before your blood pressure explodes your heart. I fully expected steam to start blowing out of his ears with the accompaniment of the sounds of a train horn.

I wanted to calm him down. But what I said almost made it worse.

"It's ok. It was only like a hundred seventy bucks or something in case we ran low on food or something May needed."

He opened his eyes and I could see my mistake instantaneously.

He took a cleansing breath.

"In case you run low on food? What does that mean? Is that something normal that happens?"

I laid my forehead on the glove box in front of me and groaned.

"Ughh... I shouldn't have said anything. I'm hardly starving."

I pinched my own stomach as proof to him that it was going to be ok. I mean I was a solid size eight. I was neither plump nor skinny and to tell the truth I wasn't really one of those girls that cared either way.

I still had my forehead pasted to the glove box when he started rubbing my back in large circles. It was as if he was consoling himself as much as me. I turned my head without it leaving the glove box and looked at him to see what damage I had done.

He mimicked my posture but his forehead was caressing the top of the steering wheel. He had his head turned towards me. He let out an enormously loud breath that made his cheeks puff out.

"One of these days..." he said "I am going to need you to tell me everything...Everything. And it will be when I know you are safe and it can't happen again. Because if you tell me now...well, I might not ever take you home again."

"Yeah? When's that gonna be?" I didn't want to doubt him; I swear it. I wanted to hang on to his every word and take them down into my being where I could hold on to them and know that they were true.

"One day...when you're mine and they can't touch you anymore."

I popped up to sitting as stiff as a Maple 2x4. I felt like I was going to hyperventilate.

"Ok, your turn...Explain." The edges of my vision were graying and my pupils could only see his mouth as he began to explain things that I would remember for the rest of my days. He sat up in his driver's side seat and turned to face me.

"J, you've got to know that I love you. You've got to know that. I know I haven't said it before, but that doesn't make it any less true. I think I've loved you since I first saw you at school before you even knew that I was alive. I know it's fast and it's crazy and believe me my friends think I'm nuts." He let out another impressive breath. Then he put his hand on the back of my neck and his thumb caressed that sensitive area under my neck where the remnants of my Mom's scratch were. His fingers were combing the hairs which grew from the back of my neck. "I feel like I've been looking for you forever. And now I've found you. I can't give you up. I want you to...No, I *need* you to marry me."

I swayed a little in my seat. I was just overwhelmed.

"I'm sorry I don't have a ring yet, but I'm saving up for it."

He misunderstood my facial expression.

I put my hands over my mouth and looked around the car just to buy myself a minute to think. I turned my head towards him slowly with my hands still on my mouth and said "Why?" The tears began again and I really didn't care this time.

He, ever so slowly, took my hands away from my face and placed them onto the sides of his face and said "Jenna, you're smart and beautiful and funny and the strongest damn girl I've ever met. You are *it* for me."

He put my hands down from his face and said, "Sorry, I know it's too quick. I just couldn't help myself. I'm surprised I lasted this long."

And it was then that my tongue made the decision for me that would prove to be the best decision of my life.

"Yes."

His eyes seemed to double in size and he said, "What?"

"Yes," I said again with a little more resolve.

"Yes what? I just need to be sure here."

I reached up around his neck and hugged him with everything I had, not caring that the stick shift was making me slant in an uncomfortable way and whispered in his ear. "Yes, Carlos, I will marry you."

He nearly squeezed the life out of me in response to my answer.

"Just remember...I said it first."

He laughed the laugh of a man who was relieved.

"Yes, I will always remember that you said it first."

We finally let go but he held me in place. I've never wanted something and been so scared of something in my whole life as I was his kiss. Please God let him kiss me.

And it was then that he did. It was soft, barely there. It was just enough for me to finally get to feel the raw heat and fullness of those lips that I had my eyes on for months. I saw balls of light behind my lids and every nerve I never knew I had came to life. His silken mouth enveloped mine and when he pulled away I moved my face forward slightly, not ready to let go yet.

He put his forehead against mine and murmured mere inches from my lips.

"I've waited to do that for a long time."

I nodded a bit in agreement. "Me, too."

"I can guarantee you that I've waited longer."

He pulled away slowly and pointed with a nodding head towards the Pier.

"Come on... I wanna see your face on the roller coaster."

I groaned and got out of the passenger side. I had to hold on to the door for a minute to steady my knees but I tried to look all passé about it.

I walked around the front of the car and his hand was already extended, waiting for me. It was a small detail to most, but to me he was offering his care and love without asking anything in return. It was a love I was going to have to get used to, a love I was learning to need.

We rode the big roller coaster and ferris wheel and then played some goofy games. He stood behind me as I tried to learn how to shoot the water at the target but I couldn't concentrate with his breath in my ear. We walked to the edge of the Pier where the older men fished in the ocean. We found a bench to sit on and I asked him about his family. I felt selfish for always talking about my problems and family. He told me about his Dad and his

Mom, she lived in another country but his Dad lived in Los Angeles. His Dad lived with a witchy step-Mom but she was nothing compared to mine. So when Carlos turned 18, he and his brother got their own apartment. His brother worked too and was 11 months older than him.

We decided on pizza for dinner and there was a little 'hole in the wall' place near the Pier. I checked the time out of habit and we still had plenty of time to get back.

We laughed and joked over a pizza with everything, even pineapple. He had taken note of my drink choice a couple of days before and ordered one for me while I was using the ladies' room. We told stories about growing up and I told funny stories about May. It was truly the first time in my life where I was liberated from my home environment and was simply me.

My eyes got wide and the realization of the day's events washed over me like a tsunami.

He saw my face and reached over to take my hand in his.

"What? What is it J?" He looked at his watch. "We're fine. It's only seven o'clock."

"You...you...I...You asked me to marry you." My eyebrows went so far up that I could feel my forehead crinkle in response.

He snorted and simply replied. "Did you forget? Don't tell me you changed your mind."

I shook my head east and west and said, "No, I just...I don't know...the reality just hit me I guess."

He let go of my hand and covered his laughing mouth with his fist. "What? You want to go right now? Come on let's go to Vegas." He moved the slightest bit pretending to leave his seat. He was laughing at himself.

"Ha ha...you're so funny.

He shrugged, "Yeah but you love it."

I looked him dead in the eye and it caused his cackling to cease.

"Yeah, I really do love you." My blush was burning like I'd stuck my face in a fireplace.

"And I love you."

We talked some more ad went for ice cream cones. He brought me home at 9:00. He didn't have to bring me home early, but I insisted since he had to catch up on homework and actually get some rest on his day off. We parked on the curb and the sound of him putting his parking brake on threw my stomach up into my throat.

He and I both simultaneously looked at the house and noted mentally that the lights were on in the house and the car was in the driveway.

He was clenching and unclenching his jaw. I could see the muscles grinding and flexing underneath the skin on the side of his face.

It was my turn to console him.

"Carlos, it's ok. I'm early. I'll go in and go to bed. It's no big deal."

"I wish..." He scrubbed his skull trim back and forth as if trying to stimulate his brain "You know you can call me if you need me. I'll come get you or take you somewhere. You know I would come and get you day or night, right?"

I smiled at my knight and returned, "I didn't, but I know now. Thank you. Believe me. I've thought about leaving. I've thought about it ten million times, but I'm determined to finish high school and they aren't going to stop me."

He nodded the tiniest bit in understanding. He was giving me that look again and I knew our second kiss was coming next. It's funny how you experience something one time and then crave it like you're addicted to it already. Then from the corner of my eye I saw the backdoor light come on, it was just a light bulb with no globe on it and the backdoor opened to reveal Medusa in full form. I did a double take as I saw the snakes for an instant. She had stepped her left foot onto the first step and had the corresponding hand on her hip. She had that look on her face that said, "Date's over."

I gave him a small smile and got out without saying a word. There was no way I could defend my childish fear of her and I was embarrassed of the power she had over me. She was still glaring as I got to the porch and moved out of my way and did a 'Vanna White' gesture to let me into the door.

"What does one do all day alone with a boy? I bet I can guess."

She slammed the back door and pushed me out of the way and stomped into her room. She was convinced that I lived the kind of life she did at my age but what she didn't know, was that I lived every day trying to be the opposite of her in every way.

I flipped off my shoes and noticed some sand in them even though we didn't walk on the beach. It warmed my heart and I rubbed my chest with my fist convincing her that it would be all right. He was mine and he loved me and not just today. He wanted me for the rest of our lives.

Chapter 14

We went out on two more dates after that. We continued to see each other every day at school. One Saturday we went out to the movies and dinner with Natalie and Oscar, the boyfriend and their 'cute as can be' baby Caroline. Natalie grabbed me by the arm on the way in to the pizza joint after the movie and slowed me down to a turtle's pace.

"He really, really loves you. You know that right?"

I smiled back at her, "Yeah, I know. I love him just as much."

"Yeah, I saw that when you bailed out of the theater that day."

I snorted, embarrassed by my own jealous behavior.

"Yeah, sorry." She laughed and it was the most lovable giggle.

She rolled her eyes and said, "Ugh, it's his fault. I told him to tell you that I wanted to meet you. He had run his mouth about you for weeks, maybe months and then he told me you were in his class on that first day."

She shook her head like the memory was that ludicrous.

"He just wouldn't shut up. So I said I wanted to see you and I wanted to bring Caroline to school anyway because some of my friends hadn't seen her. He was supposed to tell you before we got there, I promise. I wouldn't have done that to you. If that had been Oscar, Dios help me, I would've kicked him in the cajones for sure."

That got me laughing so hard. She was all of 5 feet tall. I don't think her legs could reach his 'cajones' if she stood on a chair! But dang the girl had moxie.

"It's fine. I jumped to the wrong conclusion so fast. He didn't have time to blink."

Carlos popped his head out of the front door of the restaurant smiling and said "Do we need to bring the food outside?"

She pointed her finger at him and said, "No Chistoso, we're coming. Calma te."

I gave him a look that said, 'Oh, you just got told' and he laughed and went inside.

She looked sheepish and said, "Girl, I am starving, but we can't let them know they made us hurry. Let's go and walk really slow inside."

I giggled hysterically at her walking at the rate of a slug into that restaurant that by the time we made it to the table, I had tears running down my face.

We ate and talked and he insisted that I sit on the inside of the booth and I gave him a funny 'what are you up to?' face but complied anyway. Then as we were eating, he reached out and held my right hand with his left hand. He had put me there on purpose. He knew I was left handed and he was right handed and that way we could continue to eat and still hold hands.

It was getting late and baby Caroline started to get upset towards the end of the meal. We had all ridden together so we left to go drop them off. It was out of the way but we had to bring them home first because of the baby. By the time we said our 'goodbyes' and started towards my house I thought to look and see what time it was.

I swallowed and tried to appease the meal which had risen into my throat when I looked at my watch. It was 10:47 and we were late.

"What time is it, J?" He looked worried and had already begun to drive at a faster speed before I could answer him.

I took a deep breath and shut my eyes tight as I told him. "It's 10:47."

"It's ok. We're gonna make it." I didn't know who he was trying to convince, me or him.

He started driving at a maniac's pace.

"We're not, so slow down. Getting a ticket isn't going to make it any better."

He was driving that hellacious stick shift so I couldn't hold his hand. So, I reached out and tried to rub the back of his neck while he drove. It seemed to calm him down a little.

He was full on yelling now. "I really don't care about a ticket, Jenna. I care about your psycho Mom raining hell down on you for being a few minutes late. You heard her that first time I picked you up. I mean she steals from you and she apparently hits you. Jesus, J, at this point I don't even want to bring you home at all."

I couldn't bear to look at him so worried and angry anymore so for the rest of the drive I just looked out the passenger side window and prayed. I took my hand away from his neck and twisted my fingers attempting to squeeze extra minutes out of them.

When we were almost at the turn onto my street he looked at me and smiled and said, "What has four eyes, but can't see."

"I don't know."

"Mississippi." He shrugged and pointed. There was a road sign that we were passing that said 'Mississippi Street'. I shook my head and laughed.

"Oh, that was really bad." He laughed, too, and it helped my heart, a little.

By the time we pulled into the house it was 11:13 and all the lights in the house were on including the one by the front door that we never used. It was as if they were creating a beacon for me to come home to so they could make sure I was well lighted when they punished me for the thirteen minute treachery.

I took a very deep breath and said, "Bye," I got out of the car and started walking up the driveway and before I knew it he took pace walking with me. "What the hell Carlos? I'm late already."

"No, it's my fault. I'm not going to let you take the blame." He had a great look of determination on his face.

"They don't care whose fault it is. It's always my fault, my fault alone."

"Well, get ready cause you're not alone anymore." He was a man on a mission and I fell a little deeper in love with him on that driveway.

As soon as I walked up to the back door it jolted open and revealed a very wicked woman who was extremely satisfied with the current predicament I was in.

She began her tirade. "Do you know what time it is?"

My sarcastic brain summoned up several excellent answers for her question. 'Bedtime? Break time? Nap time? Tea Time? Hammer Time?' But I refrained from putting fuel on the fire. I had to clamp down on my tongue with my teeth not to say it.

Carlos stepped in between her and I and the surprise of his actions made her step back a few small paces.

"I'm so sorry. It's my fault she's late. I had to bring my friends home first and it took longer than expected. Please don't blame Jenna. Blame me."

I was looking between them watching it all unfold as if I wasn't a player but just a spectator. It was fascinating.

"Oh, don't worry." She smiled her infamous fake smile. "I do blame you. But I also blame her and you standing there trying to save her from the consequences isn't helping Mister Save Jenna From Her Mean Hateful Mother."

He looked at me and I saw him deciding what his best move was. He finally slowly walked away. His look of defeat crushed me. He got in his car and my Mom and I were still standing there gawking as he drove away. I looked up and met her cold steely gaze.

"Get your ass in this house and we're going to have a little discussion about responsibility and the price you pay when you don't follow the rules. And don't wake your sister up either. She's been up all night crying for you."

That was a low blow and she knew it. May knew where I was. I had told her everything about Carlos in one of our secret closet meetings. And even if she didn't know she wasn't one of those toddlers who cried all night for something they wanted.

"Ok," I said and I went inside and there was already a chair in the middle of the room waiting for me. If it had one of those swinging light bulbs and a cup of stale coffee it would've been sooooo **CSI**. I snickered to myself at the thought. I knew what I was in for. I had gotten one of these all night lectures after I was late coming home from the library because the public bus on my route had broken down. I was in for a multiple hour lecture where I was expected to listen intently and at the end I would be told what they were taking from me. My Step-Dad, of course, pulled up a chair on the side of the room to watch the show.

I sat in the antique looking chair and pulled my legs up to get comfortable. I let out a deep sigh and she stood up and so it began....

"Do you know what kind of girls stay out at all hours of the night?"

Her droll voice and berating and belittling continued for hours. *For the love of all that is holy, it was only 13 minutes.* I wanted to scream it, but I was paralyzed in her presence. I couldn't justify it or even understand it. It was an unconscious reaction.

I made the mistake of glancing at the clock about a quarter after 12 in the morning and she got right in my face and said "Oh now you can look at the clock?"

The interrogation lasted for about fifteen minutes after that and she finally sat down and said. "So...here are your consequences. Two weeks, no dates. And if I find out that you're calling him from work or seeing him when you're supposed to be at work I will make you quit your job. You go to school and work and that's it. And if you get caught with him during the next two weeks I will make sure you never see the little bastard again. We clear?"

I was exhausted mentally, physically and emotionally and I just nodded to her.

She said, "You did it to yourself Jenna. I set the rules and you made a choice not to follow them. I can't believe you made us stay up all night and do this."

I just nodded again like the idiot that I was.

"Just go to bed. You look like hell and I'm tired of looking at your face."

I went to my bed and collapsed; clothes and all. I didn't even get under the covers I flung the part that hung over my bed over my legs and passed out.

Chapter 15

That Sunday I slept in most of the day. My brains hurt and if there was such a thing...my soul was tired. I lay in my bed and let myself dream and wonder. I'd never allowed myself to let the dreamed up plans go too far. I didn't want to get my hopes up. But today, it was allowed and encouraged.

I needed to find a way out of this life. I was used to it and I could take it. I had lived with it for so long that I was numb to it all.

But Carlos wasn't. He wasn't used to it and he didn't understand it and I never wanted him to. I wanted him to be as separated from this dysfunction as possible. And I never wanted to see that look of defeat in his eyes ever again.

I sat up swiftly in bed and concreted my resolve. I was now keeping my eyes wide open for my chance. It had to be a chance that got not just me, but Carlos and me far away from them. As far as possible.

I did a ton of laundry that day and folded all of May and my clothes. We reorganized her dresser and put all of her clothes that were too small for her in a bag. I would have to buy her some more with my next paycheck. I then reorganized her Petshops by species and re-arranged her furniture in her hand-me-down dollhouse.

For the rest of the afternoon I drowned myself in music. I had my earbuds way too loud and several times I wondered if I would still be able to hear when I was old. Then the greatest thought occurred to me. When I got old...he would be there with me. Carlos would be with me when I got old. I smiled to myself and changed my genre of music to words that reinforced my love for him.

Monday arrived and I was not looking forward to telling Carlos that we wouldn't be able to go anywhere together for two weeks. I knew that he would blame himself no matter how much I tried to convince him otherwise. I didn't want to see his sadness again.

I trudged up the stairs and turned to make my way to my locker where I was sure he was waiting. I craned my head around the corner. I spotted my locker right away but he wasn't there. I looked down the hall but didn't see him down there either. Him standing at my locker in the morning had become such a constant that it worried me that he wasn't there today. Especially after the way he had left on Saturday night. The self-doubt and doubt of my previous resolve wrapped its black fingers around my heart. It was as if in mere seconds I had forgotten the words which were spoken, the love that was exchanged.

I dropped off half of my books in my locker and begrudgingly made my way to homeroom. While walking between buildings I saw him. He was getting out of his car in quite a hurry and as he closed his driver's side door, he was looking towards the gate. The Coach of the soccer team was apparently on gate duty today and he was edging the chain link closer to meeting its partner as fast as he could. Carlos barely squeezed through and after straightening himself met my gaze. We both looked in the air as the bell rang.

I looked down and continued to walk towards my homeroom. Honestly, I didn't know what to say to him and really I was waiting for him to say that it was all too much. I was waiting for him to admit that I wasn't worth the fight, wasn't worth the hassle. Wasn't worth the time or energy needed to deal with my drama. I let these thoughts drag me down into a depressing swamp and there is where I stayed for the rest of the day.

I kept my head down as I made my way between classes. I saw him in his usual spot between third period and fourth period but I cut through the herd and made my way up the stairs as fast as I could.

For the first time in a long time I was reluctant about going to sixth period. I hardly ever skipped but it was tempting today. I walked as slowly as possible and slid through the door as the bell was blaring in my ears. I made my way to my desk, sat down with my bag on top of the desk and put my forehead on it.

Mr. Escobar got in front of the class and got everyone's attention. He said that if we wanted to we were free to go to the school library for the rest of the period since he had to reorganize the classroom since he didn't want to work on it over the summer.

I jumped out of my seat and nearly ran to the door. I thought I could make a clean getaway, go somewhere where my walls could be firmly in place without anyone trying to knock them down or get in.

Burly arms encircled my waist and he whispered in my ear, "Don't do this, Jenna. Don't shut me out. I'm here and we're going to talk…now." He took my hand and guided me through campus to the library and back to sit at a table which was hidden behind the biographies.

I sat down sideways in the smooth wooden chair and he sat down opposite me and looked overwrought with emotion. Which one it was, I was about to find out.

I opened my mouth to start and then closed it. Opened it again and closed it again without a peep coming out.

"Tell me what happened." He took my chin in his hand and turned my face back and forth. I knew what he was looking for but obliged him.

"I just got a very, very long lecture and then they told me that I can't go out with you for two weeks. I'm not supposed to call you or see you unless it's in class and if I get caught seeing you, they are saying they will stop me from seeing you at all."

He let out a big sigh and moved his chair closer to mine.

"Jenna, it took everything in me to leave you there. I just thought the longer I stayed, the worse it would be for you. It killed me to leave you there at their mercy. But she didn't....I mean I don't see any..."

I smiled to reassure him, "No, it was emotional interrogation this time."

"That's not funny." He was rubbing my arms now from my elbows to my wrists and back again.

I shrugged. "I guess we'll only see each other in school for a couple of weeks and they won't let me talk to you on the phone."

"You mean they won't let you talk to me on their house phone, right"

"No, I meant that won't let me talk to you on my Bat Phone."

"Ok, ok, cut it out smart ass."

I opened my mouth in a wide 'O' and tried to look truly offended. I even put my hand over my heart for effect.

"Well, that was just rude, Sir." He chuckled and the rumble melted my heart.

"They didn't say anything about talking to me on a cell phone did they?"

"No... but that's probably because...um...yeah...I don't have a cell phone."

"I think you do."

"Oh, yeah, where is it?"

"Right here." He pulled out a phone from his bag and handed it to me.

"Oh, no...you can't give me your phone. I didn't even know you had a phone." At this point I was waving my hands, palms out, in the air like I was directing some kind of small aircraft.

"It's not my phone..." He pulled an identical phone from his bag. "This is my phone."

I pawed at his bag jokingly, "Dang, what else is in there?"

He rolled his eyes at me. "This phone already has my number programmed in. I want you to call me anytime you want to or *need* to. OK? Just keep the ringer off."

I surrendered when I looked into his eyes. How could I not?

"Ok"

"Good. That's where I was this morning."

"Huh..." That's all I could get out.

"So...you want to tell me why you've been avoiding me all day? Ack..." He put his hand out when I opened my mouth in protest. "Don't even try to deny it, J."

I started in a whisper because I was now thoroughly disgusted with myself for ever doubting him or us.

"I don't know. I thought maybe...maybe I wasn't worth the trouble. I mean my life is a mess and my parents are...Hell I don't know what they are, but it's trouble. I mean if I were you I wouldn't..." My mouth apparently had truth diarrhea today.

He closed his eyes and did that anger management thing where I could swear he was mentally counting to ten. His knee started bobbing, too. He cut me off before I could finish my ridiculous explanation.

"Please don't finish...please." His eyes were still closed. "Remember the Pier?" He could see my face as I processed a snarky come back.

"Dumb question. Look, I...Love...You. Not just that night on the Pier or when things are going good. We don't have to deal with your parents for very much longer. After you graduate, you can get out of there and never look back, right?"

"Yeah...I can." He smiled.

"Ok, so we deal with them the best we can until then. We..."

He emphasized his point by giving my forearms a gentle squeeze. It was then that I looked down and saw his tattoo. The one that I noticed the very first time I saw him. I rubbed my thumb across it and said, "Is that your name? It's kinda fuzzy."

"That, yeah. I got it done when I was twelve at a place that wasn't exactly a legal tattoo place. And then I grew up and it kinda grew with me." He smiled with a far off look. "My Mom beat my butt so bad...I didn't sit down right for a week."

"I don't blame her. But it's kinda hot."

He locked eyes with me and said, "You think my tattoos are hot?"

I blushed the entire spectrum of red and answered breathlessly.

"Yeah, I do."

"Well, wait until you see the rest of them."

I raised my hands to cover my blush and hide but he caught my hands.

"Don't you dare. I love it when I make you blush. And I make you blush a lot. It's not like you can hide it."

We both laughed and I slapped his outer thigh to make him stop laughing at me.

The bell rang and we both stood up at the same time. Our mouths and faces were inches, no, centimeters from each other and I could smell the Aspen trees and cinnamon waft towards me, wrapping my senses in pleasure.

The librarian came around the corner and cleared her throat very loudly. I glared at her but Carlos put his hands on each side of my waist and drew me out of my annoyance with her.

He took my hand and led me out of the library and towards the parking lot. I cocked my head to the side and said, "I've got to get the bus."

"Nope, not today. They switched my days and I have tonight off." He saw my alarm and said while aggressively rubbing the back of his neck with his other hand. "Look, I'll drop you off a few blocks from your house and you can walk home, ok? I'm just....I'm just not ready to let you go yet today."

I just stood there like a zombie for a few seconds and almost teared up.

I relented and said, "You take care of me."

He nodded and then laughed while he wrapped his arm around my shoulders and kissed my temple. "I always will, J. I thought we had covered this. You're kinda slow. Jeez."

I reached out and tried to push his waist away and wrangle out of his shoulder hold at the same time.

I balked at him, "Oooooh back to the insults, ok."

He just continued laughing while we walked to his car. Most of the cars were gone by then and he walked me to the passenger's side of the car. He took my bag from off of my shoulder and put both of our bags in the back seat. He looked around the parking lot and then back to me. He took a few slow steps towards me and I backed away only to find that his car was his accomplice in his devilish scheme.

My eyes widened at his expression and I blurted out.

"What are you thinking?"

He stepped dangerously close and his right leg stepped tentatively then confidently in between my legs. He put both hands out on the car behind me on either side of my ribcage. He crept closer and closer until I thought I would melt just by his proximity. My breaths were coming out in shallow huffs and anyone in a ten mile radius could probably hear them. He leaned down methodically and slowly to the point of torture. He kissed me gently on my neck right below my earlobe, I felt his breath on my neck and in my hair and I shivered. He whispered in my ear.

"Baby, you don't want to know what I'm thinking."

"Carlos, you're killing me."

He continued his whispering assault, "Mmmm...you're just feeling a little of what I go through all the time with you."

I was caught off guard a little at this new stage in our relationship.

I reached out a hand and tugged at his goatee.

"I had no idea. I mean you've said I was..." I couldn't make myself say the words.

"Well..." he pulled back and smiled at me, "I must not have made myself clear. I'll have to fix that. Plus...You started it."

"When was that? I missed it."

"You're the one who said my tattoo was hot. Your fault." He looked down at my lips and I licked them and then my gaze floated to his lips. He was still looking at my lips when he said, "Man, I want to kiss you like crazy."

"Yeah...you should...um...in 2 weeks."

"Damn..." He put his forehead on my shoulder. "I'm sorry again. We'll make up for it."

He gave me a peck on the very corner of my mouth and said, "I guess I'd better get you home...or 2 blocks from home."

"Yeah"...I was still breathless.

He drove me back towards my house and dropped me 2 away so no one would be the wiser. I walked home and walked through the back door determined that I wasn't going to let them get to me.

When I got home my Mom had the front closet emptied, which was really weird because all of her 'hidey bills' were stored in there. She had piles of suitcases laid out in the middle of the living room floor and she had half of her clothes out draping the couch. It looked like one of those men on t.v. who stands outside of the fitting room while his wife throws out the clothes she doesn't want. She was running into her bedroom with this goofy ass grin on her face. I grinned too because all of these cockamamie scenarios went through my head.

She found out that the circus is taking Medusa/June Cleaver acts. She's hit the big time!

The local Pawn Shop is paying double for all luggage brought in. Today only!

She burst back into the room.

"Jenna, I have some great news for you."

I almost wanted to point to myself and say, "Me?"

"What?"

"Well...Great news for all of us. Today we bought 4 tickets for us to go to Louisiana on vacation. Isn't that great?" She was overly excited.

Where would they get money to buy airplane tickets? And vacation, seriously, they don't even work.

"Oh, yeah? When?" I tried to sound excited, but it came out sounding like a pop star during an uncomfortable interview.

"Two days after you graduate. You should call your Dad later and tell him that we're coming. I'm sure he'd love to see you. You are actually on a flight the day before we leave. They only had three seats left on our plane."

I frowned a little because she hated my real Dad's guts. She usually referred to my real Dad as 'him'…It made me think of 'someone who shall not be named.'

"Yeah…ok…I will call him after I get home from work." I walked out of the room in a major state of confusion.

I put my bag down and switched to my purse and put everything I needed in it, including my new secret cell phone.

I walked through the living room and her mood was the same but she said as I tried to walk through the minefield of stuff on the floor, "Jenna, let's not forget…2 weeks from Saturday. You wouldn't want to mess that up right?"

"I know, Mom."

I shut the door behind me and began my walk to the music store.

As soon as I got past the freeway, I looked back to make sure that the coast was clear. I didn't see anyone so I took my new cell phone out. I had seen other people using their cell phones on the bus and at school so I figured it out quickly.

"Hello?" he answered.

"Hey. I'm walking to work so I thought I'd call you. I know I just saw you   but.."

He snorted on the other end.

"I'm glad you called Jenna. How long is your walk to work?"

"It's twelve blocks."

"Twelve blocks...well...at least we have a while to talk."

"Yep. So...I walked in the house and guess what my Mom tells me?"

"There's no telling. I don't even know your Mom well, but I can't stand her already."

That made me laugh harder than I had in a long time. I could barely stop laughing to talk to him anymore.

"Oh, you have no idea. You've only known about her antics for a few months. I've had to deal with them for 18 years!"

He chuckled, "Thank God...although, no never mind...I would've known you."

He cleared his throat and said, "So, tell me what she said."

"She said she bought the whole family tickets to go visit Louisiana. I'm supposed to leave 2 days after graduation. But supposedly they only had 3 tickets on their airplane the next day. So I leave 1 day before them."

The line stayed silent so long that I pulled the phone away from my ear to see if I was still on the call.

"Carlos?"

"So, you get to see your Dad. That's good. How long will you be gone?"

"I think a week." I had forgotten to ask that.

"So you leave in about six weeks?"

"Yeah."

"Well we still have prom before you go."

"We do?" I asked.

"Actually...No, I want to marry you, but I'm going to take someone else to prom. Is that ok? I mean I'll see you there. It's no big deal."

"Ahem... Who is the smart ass now?"

He laughed, "Ugh...I wish I was with you right now so I could ask you the right way. But ...will you go with me to prom Jenna?"

"Awww...of course I will."

By this time I was getting close to the store.

"Hey, I'm almost to the store so I have to go."

"OK…if you feel like it, call me on your way home."

" I will. I love you."

"I love you too, J. I'll talk to you later."

"Bye." I hung up and walked into the store.

Mr. Cannon informed me that the music was a bigger priority today than the vacuuming and dusting. "Little Lady, that stack of music in there is higher than Mount Fuji."

I giggled, "OK, I'm on it."

I went towards the back, but remembered to tell him about my trip.

"Oh, Mr. Cannon, I forgot to tell you that my Mom planned a trip to Louisiana for us it's in about six weeks. I think I'll be gone for a week."

"Do you know the exact dates?"

"Yes, I'm pretty sure of them."

"Ok, well mark them on the employee calendar."

"Yes, Sir."

I went to work and he was underestimating that stack of music I had to re-shelve. It was enormous.

I got off work at seven instead of six thirty and started to make my way home. I called Carlos and talked to him all the way until I got to the freeway. I walked home and when I got there what had started as Mrs. Happy Travelling Lady was now a heap on the floor and resembled more of a weepy mess.

"What happened?" I asked her.

"I was just laying everything out to go to on our vacation and I realized...ugh...all I have are old clothes to wear."

I stood there stupefied. What did she want *me* to do?

"Jenna, do you have any money from your paycheck so I can buy something decent to wear?"

I was furious.

"Mom, I would give you my money. I would. But I had it all in my top drawer and I went to get some of it last weekend and it was gone."

She looked fake-shocked. "Oh, my goodness, I hope someone didn't break in to our house while we were gone."

"I hope they did."

"Why?" She was such a poor actress.

"Because the alternative makes me sick to my stomach."

And with that I walked off into my room. I did some homework. We didn't have much since we were ending the end of the year, but I did it anyway.

I called my Dad and he was excited for me to come and visit. I also had a Step-Mom and sister Sophia whom I hadn't seen since she was about six weeks old. I gave him the dates and he assured me he was going to pick me up at the airport.

I played with May a little and when my Mom made supper there was conveniently only enough for the three of them. She said I was on my own for dinner. When she said that, she was talking about a lot more than dinner. I was on my own....period. Little did she know.

Chapter 15

The next day when I arrived at school there was something big going on. I had to read the flyers in the hall to see what the uproar was about.

Remember Seniors!

Graduation Pictures on the Bleachers During 6th Period.

Cap and Gown Mandatory.

I hadn't received any notice about my cap and gown. I know that I put the money order and size specifications in an envelope and put it in the mail. I did it myself, so I know it was done. I couldn't afford a class ring, but I had to have a cap and gown to walk at the ceremony. I made my way to the Senior Center where everything from yearbooks to key chains and everything in between could be purchased. I gave the lady at the counter my name and as she was checking the records for cap and gown purchases I looked around the room and was overwhelmed by all of the Senior goods.

She cleared her throat and I smiled at her waiting for her to tell me where my cap and gown were.

"I'm sorry, Jenna. We don't have a record of an order. When did you mail it?"

"I mailed it the day after it was given to us."

"I'm not sure what happened. But without a cap and gown you'll have to miss the class picture today." She gave me a pity smile and I shrugged it off like I didn't care.

I know I mailed my order.

I didn't mind missing the picture. It wasn't that big of a deal. But now I had to find out how to get a cap and gown before graduation.

I got to my locker and I was in my own world until I got about a foot in front of him.

"Hey," I said and before I knew what I was doing had my face against his hard warm chest and my arms around his middle. He didn't hesitate to put his arms around my shoulders and his chin rested atop my head. It was a need I didn't even have to think about. I just needed his comfort.

"What happened?" he said and as he spoke his chin bobbed against the top of my head. He didn't let go of me.

"Ughhh....I'm just aggravated. The cap and gown pictures are today and I hadn't gotten mine yet. But I know I mailed the order and the money order with it. And I went to the Senior Center and they say they have no record of my order. So now I have to find one before graduation and...well...I'm just pissed."

He chuckled at that and I could hear and feel the rumbling of his chest under my ear which was still pasted to his chest.

"You didn't turn your order into the Senior Center?" he asked

"No, I got a money order and mailed it from the house...."

I looked up at him and we were on the same page already.

No words were necessary. I closed my eyes and put my head back down.

"We still have time to get you another one. They still have order forms. I saw them the other day when I was getting the prom tickets."

"You already bought them?" I was surprised.

"Yeah, I bought them the first day they went on sale. Let's go order your cap and gown."

"I can't. I have to wait until I get paid again."

"I will pay for it...Don't start, J. I'm happy to do it, really."

"Ok, let's order it tomorrow, ok? I just came out of there."

He chuckled again and kissed the top of my head on my hair.

"Sounds good."

He squeezed me tight as the bell rang and ripped us from our happiness.

"See you in Drama?"

"Yup," I answered as I shoved my books in my locker.

The day didn't get much better but sure as heck didn't get worse. Sixth period came and went twice as quickly as I wanted it to, and I wouldn't get to talk to him tonight because he had to work and I did too.

The rest of the week went by like a flash and before I knew it the weekend was upon me. Carlos had ordered my cap and gown the same day as the graduation pictures. He had asked the teacher on duty to help him guess my size. Thankfully she knew who I was. He paid for it in full and had even paid for a faster processing time.

We had only talked at school this week as our work and sleep schedules kept us from it. I missed him severely. By next Sunday I would be free, but I didn't know if he would be off of work that day so I didn't get my hopes up. *Who am I kidding? My hopes are so high; they are stuck in the atmosphere.*

Saturday after I got home from work my Mom was back to Medusa again. She was scrambling around the house complaining about not having enough clothes and about me being broke. Even if I wasn't broke, I wouldn't give it to her. *Hasn't she taken enough from me?*

I went to clean my room and do some laundry for the week, since I didn't have anything else to do. I cleaned out our closet and got the biggest hug from May because I found her beloved, very rare, giraffe Pet Shop toy. I nearly laughed myself to death when she asked me if I knew exactly how rare it was. I told her I didn't and she said, "You just saved my collection." That made me laugh to no end. That kid was a trip.

I went to put another load of clothes into the dryer and one more load of towels into the washer. We had run out of laundry detergent, of course. So I went to tell my Mom that I was going to get some but I couldn't find her. I scoured the house and the 'office' and couldn't find her anywhere. I went back to my room and asked May if she had seen her.

"Yes, she's gone," she said as the other Pet Shops were so happy that the giraffe had come back to play with them.

"Where'd she go?" I asked.

"Dad said she got something in the mail and he gave it to her. Then she started dancing like this."

She got up and started waving her hands in the air and knocking her knees together and she twirled her hips around like she was balancing a hula hoop.

"What was it?" I asked her.

She shrugged her shoulders and went back to playing. The giraffe and the hippo were fighting already.

"Well, May, we have to go get some more laundry soap. Get your shoes on Sprite."

"Do I get a candy bar?" She pressed her hands together in prayer.

"Depends on how fast you get your shoes on."

That got her going. She got her flip flops on in record time and was ready to go.

On the way to the nearest store I thought about calling Carlos with my phone but I didn't know if he was at work and the way May just jumped for candy I really didn't trust her not to be bribed.

We got to the store and I bought laundry detergent and some more dryer sheets just in case. May picked a

Twix bar and I promised her she could eat it after some dinner. On the way home from the drug store was a little place that had chicken strips that May liked. I bought her a basket with fries and we made our way home. The whole way I tried to figure out what Mom had gotten in the mail that made her do that crazy dance. It was probably another random check or something.

We got home and whatever was in that envelope had been spent. It must've been one heck of a check. There were bags and clothes and shoes everywhere. There was some for him, some for her and even some stuff for May. There were also new luggage bags, new makeup and everything in between. Whatever kind of check this was, I wanted one.

Mom came out of the bedroom in what was obviously a new outfit complete with shoes and jewelry. She looked like she belonged front and center at a real estate conference, the cheesy kind of realtors whose faces were on park benches that homeless people slept on.

She did a spin and said, "Well, lookin' good right?"

"Mmmmhmmm," was all I could muster up.

May just said, "Yup," and dug in to her chicken strips and fries.

I went into the kitchen and got her some apple juice and set it on the table.

I walked back through the living room and tiptoed through the mess and bags. I must've looked like a football player going through those tire exercises.

I got to my room and my Mom was on my heels.

Her fake smile was in full force.

"Jenna, I hope you aren't upset that we didn't buy you anything. I really don't know what size you've gotten up to now and I'm not really sure what would flatter your kind of...shape." She waved her newly braceleted hand in the air and continued, "Anyway, you are always shopping and buying clothes so you don't need anything. I never get to go shopping." She pouted out her bottom lip because she was really, really sad...hardly.

"It's really great, Mom. You're right. I am *always* getting all kinds of stuff. Last month I bought twelve whole dollars worth of clothes. I'm such a high maintenance diva." I rolled my eyes dramatically.

She was on me like white on rice. She grabbed me by my wrists and got into my face and screamed, "Don't you ever talk to me like that again you sack of shit. Do you hear me? You think because you've got a boy treating you nice right now that you're better than everyone? What do you think he wants in return for all of that sweetness, huh? I bet I can guess. And clean up your damned room!"

She grabbed my jaw and shoved me to the other side of the room. I opened my mouth to question her, but she had answered my question before I even started. She reached behind my dresser...A dresser that my real Dad had built for me before I was born and pushed it to the floor spilling out everything, everywhere. She opened my closet and threw everything I owned out on the floor.

"Jenna, really at your age? Get this mess cleaned up now."

I scrubbed my face for a good five minutes before I got up to clean the mess up. When I did my wrists barely held me up. That Medusa must be lifting weights because they hurt and there were finger shaped bruises like bracelets marring my skin.

I picked up the dresser and returned it to its rightful place and if I thought my wrists hurt before, they really hurt now. As I did all of the dresser drawers fell out and I had made a bigger mess than before.

I spent the rest of the afternoon cleaning up the mess and before I went to bed I had to take a couple of Tylenol for my wrists.

I spent Sunday laying low. Prom was in two weeks and I didn't want a shiner to be one of my accessories.

Everyone else was still relishing in their new purchases so I walked outside late in the afternoon and sat on my back steps just to get some fresh air. My next door neighbor Rebecca was sitting on her front porch. She was rocking in an ancient rocking chair and looking through some kind of fashion magazine. I had talked to her once on Halloween when I took May Trick or Treating. She was dressed up as a ballerina that year. Rebecca had complimented her on her costume and told us that she worked in movies making costumes. I didn't want to disturb her so I just sat there for a while watching the cars go by.

She got up and went inside after a while and reappeared shortly after with two glasses of lemonade. She leaned over the railing and she smiled. Lord that woman had some big teeth. And when she talked her teeth impeded her speech. But she was nice enough, though I wasn't sure if she was the 'tattle tale' neighbor or not.

"Hey, Jenna, I fixed you a glass of lemonade, too. Why don't you come and sit with me for a while?"

Maybe I could pick her brain, see if she was the culprit.

"Yeah, sure, thank you."

I walked down our driveway and around her porch to get to the stairs which led to the chairs. They were white wicker with the loudest Hawaiian print ever on them.

"So, how's school, Jenna?"

Ugh, I hate when people ask me how school's going. I don't know why, it just seems like a question that pops out of their brains without thinking. Like they see a younger person and their mouths form the words without their knowledge.

"Um...It's fine. Thanks. I'll be graduating in about four and a half weeks."

"Oh...that's wonderful. So you must be gearing up for prom, right?"

"Yeah, I mean, I have a date and he has the tickets, but I don't have a dress yet or anything."

"Oh, I bet your date is that young man who I've seen picking you up and dropping you off from school, right? I told your Mom that he was such a gentleman and walked you to the door and everything and so cute. Wooooh!"

She started fanning herself and then it hit me.

You...you horse toothed costuming wench! You're the one who almost got my teeth knocked down my throat!

"Jenna, are you ok?"

"Yeah, um, you telling my Mom didn't go over so well."

She nearly jumped from her chair. "What?"

She sat down further into her chair again, "I told your Mom exactly what I just told you that he walked you to the door and he opened your car door for you. You didn't get in trouble for it right? Oh, no! I mean I've heard noises from your house but I just thought your parents fought a lot."

She dropped her face into her hands and I thought she was going to sob right there. I reached out and touched her arm to get her attention.

"Hey, no, it's ok. No matter what you said sometimes I just...well...trouble finds me, you know?"

"Jenna, I'm so sorry, I didn't mean anything by it."

"It's ok Ms. Rebecca, really, I know you didn't mean anything."

"Please, Jenna, it's just Rebecca."

We sat there for a few minutes more and sipped our lemonade. I felt bad for telling her that I got in trouble, she looked like she was upset about it still.

Suddenly she got a huge grin on her face and it scared the ever loving crap out of me because it was unexpected and because...well...the teeth.

"I know how I can make it up to you, Jenna! I have the best idea."

"Uhhhh...ok? Shoot."

"How about I make your prom dress for you?" I opened my mouth to tell her she didn't have to make up for anything but she continued, shushing me with her hand up.

"Now I won't take no for an answer. What we'll do is next weekend we will go fabric shopping Downtown. I have a wholesale license so I can buy fabric really cheap. We can pick out your fabric and I will have some pictures of different styles of dresses you can choose from. Trust me, if you find a dress you like I can sew it. And when we get back I can take your measurements and sew it up lickety split. You'll have a one of a kind dress for sure and certain."

The whole time, every time she made a point, she was clapping and stomping her feet. I couldn't tell her 'no', she was too darn excited to turn her down.

"Really? You would do that for me?"

I teared up. I was coming to realize that the best people, the ones who treat you the best and want you happy, at least in my case, are not the ones in your family.

"Yes!" She jumped up and hugged the life out of me.

I was squealing with her until over her shoulder Medusa came out in full swing. She straightened her posture and plastered that horrible fake smile to her mouth and waved at us.

"Rebecca, so nice to see you! What's all the excitement about, hmmm?"

Rebecca turned around and gave my Mom not so enthusiastic response.

"Well, Jenna here was telling me that prom is coming up and I told her that I didn't have anything going right now. I leave for Japan in a month, but until then I am free. So I offered to make Jenna's prom dress."

At this moment I wished Carlos or a friend were with me so I could poke them in the ribs with my elbow and say, "Ooooohhhh, watch this, watch what she's gonna do!"

My Mom was in a conundrum. She probably wanted to knock me into next week for even thinking about prom, but she was in front of the neighbor and she didn't want to give anyone a bad impression.

I snorted at the comedy of it all and my Mom's eyes darted directly to mine.

"Well, Jenna, we hadn't spoken about prom. Thank you Rebecca; that would be so kind of you to make her dress. When are you two going to get the fabric?"

Oh, here we go. Rebecca doesn't even see it coming.

"Next Saturday, right Jenna?" I smiled and nodded.

My Mom was seething; her jaws were clenching and unclenching.

I wanted to scream 'Na na na boo boo, you can't say anything mean.' Probably not the most mature thing, but I get my kicks where I can.

"Well" She batted her eyes and a chill ran down my spine. "I would love to go too and see what Jenna has in mind."

Rebecca was clapping again. She was apparently oblivious to what my Mom was doing.

"Oh, yay! We'll have a girl's day and pick fabric and have lunch and..."

She continued clapping and planning while Medusa and I had a stare off. She smirked at me and I knew that she had won this round. She'd probably convince Rebecca to make me a Moomoo out of the same Hawaiian fabric as these hideous chairs on her porch just to spite me.

I cleared my throat to end the conversation so I could go inside. I hugged Rebecca and thanked her again. She beamed and I pitied her because she didn't know what she was doing by letting Mom come with us.

When I got inside I looked in on May who was reading some kind of book about a spider family.

It was almost eight o'clock and I decided to go ahead and go to sleep and hoped that tomorrow would be better.

Chapter 16

Monday was Monday but at least I got out of the house. Instead of my regular route to my locker, I took the long way around. I had a plan. I walked slowly towards my locker and Carlos was there, he was so predictable. And I loved him for it. He was leaning his right shoulder against my locker and was looking in the direction that I usually walked in from. His backpack was on the floor by his feet.

I snuck up behind him and snaked my arms around his middle and said, "Waitin for somebody?"

He hugged my arms tighter around his waist and then turned around to face me.

He reached down and put his arms around my waist and picked me up the small distance where we were the same height. My arms made their way around his neck and he held on to me like he never had before.

I pulled back and said, "What's wrong? Did you miss me that much?"

I giggled, but he didn't.

He pulled me back to him again and whispered desperately in my ear, "Yes Jenna, I missed you so much I didn't know if I could stand one more minute without you. Three days is too much."

I felt awful for picking on him about it.

I returned his whisper, "I'm sorry. I missed you, too, so much."

I kissed him below his earlobe like he had done in the parking lot last week and I could hear his swift intake of breath and feel him shuddering next to me.

He put me down gently and still whispering said, "You can't do that to me here, J. Wait until next weekend. Save them up for then."

"Why?" I felt like I was such a dork for always asking this.

"Because when you kiss me, I want to kiss you back and not in front of strangers."

I giggled, "Oh, in front of your friends?"

He chuckled and the bell started to ring. He picked up his bag and walked past me and just when I thought he was going to leave me like that he came up behind me. His hands started at the top of my ribs and worked their way down as he spoke. And his mouth...his lips were barely grazing the outside of my ear as he said "I want you alone, J, with your mouth on mine and trust me, the last thing you will be doing is giggling."

Now it was my turn to gasp and he gave me a peck on the side of my face and walked off, free as a bird, like he hadn't just stoked a small fire inside me right there in the middle of the hallway.

I had to shake my head to clear it before I could even walk to class. School was not going to be fun today with all of the thoughts he had just put in my head. That was a fact.

~ ~

Waiting to see him in between classes was getting harder and harder since that was the only time I got to see him. It was ridiculous and I couldn't wait for my 'grounding' to be over with. I wondered if he had to work next Sunday since I was free after Saturday again.

I got to sixth period and went to my usual seat. Mr. Escobar had a new bulletin board up and it had pictures of all of us in the play. I tried not to look at it. I just wanted to forget being in front of all of those people and here he was parading it around.

Carlos came in just as the bell was ringing and did some kind of slap, clap, hand shake thing with his friends and then came to sit by me.

Without my permission at the very sight of him, my blush made herself known and it wasn't just in my cheeks. Everything was engulfed in the blush from my temples to my chest.

He tried to hide the fact that he noticed immediately and sat down while clearing his throat and smiled at me.

"Why so red, Jenna?" I closed my eyes and shook my head. Like he didn't know why.

"Wouldn't you like to know?" I raised my eyebrow and smiled at him.

He shifted in his seat and I wondered if I made him uncomfortable or nervous or something altogether different.

He shook his head as if reading my thoughts, "So, what are you up to on Sunday?"

I inhaled through my nose and shrugged, trying to act so nonchalant about the whole thing. He wasn't the only one who could play this game.

"I don't know. Depends."

"Depends on what?" He was playing along too now.

"Depends on what you're doing on Sunday."

"How early can I pick you up?" I smiled wide. They were words from heaven.

"Do you have to work on Saturday night?"

"Yeah, but it's ok. I can sleep in the afternoon or something."

"Oh no you don't. Get some sleep and then pick me up about *two*. Is that ok?"

He let out this sound that was a mix of a groan and a growl.

"Noon"

"One, you need to sleep."

"Are you sure she won't let us go out on Saturday?"

I sighed, "No, she won't, plus now I have plans..."

He stuck his bottom lip out again and it was all I could look at. I couldn't wait until I could feel them on mine again.

"I'm going to pick out the fabric and the dress design for my prom dress."

That took him out of his funk and quick.

"You're having it made? I thought I was gonna get to buy it for you."

"Awww, thank you. I never expected you to pay for it. I've got it. Anyway, you don't get to see it beforehand. The lady that lives next door is going to make it for me. She's a costume designer for movies."

"Really? That's lucky for you. Any hints?"

"Actually I don't even know what I want yet. She's going to let me look at some pictures of dresses and she said if she has a picture of it she can sew it. She must be really good."

He looked surprised and happy at the same time. "Wow, she must be."

"So what are we doing on Sunday?" I was eager for something to look forward to.

He shook his head. "Oh, no, you keep secrets, so I'm keeping this secret."

He thought he had me, that I was going to confess what color and dress I had in mind. But, he was wrong.

"Ok, that's fine." Class was about to end and I picked up my bag to get ready to go.

He smiled and picked up my hand that was lying on my desk and played with my fingers. I had worn a long sleeved shirt on purpose to hide the bruises on my wrists. They were turning yellowish but he still would notice and I didn't want to add any worry to his plate. He looked like he had never seen fingers before.

"So, I'm off today. Can I take you home?"

"You can take me almost home."

He laughed at the same time the bell rang.

"I'll take what I can get, J."

He drove me home the long way around and about two blocks from my house he pulled onto the side of the road to let me out.

"Jenna, I..." He let out an awful sounding sigh "I just miss spending time with you. I see you in school but it's like it's not enough anymore. You'll never be late again, trust me, because I can't take this."

I reached up and tugged on his goatee.

"I know. It's hard. Sunday, ok? Let's just countdown to Sunday."

He took my hand from his goatee and pressed my fingers to his lips and kissed them. Even though I was trying not to I winced from him touching my wrist and he caught on instantly. His hardened eyes looked at me and I just looked down. I knew I had been caught.

He held my hand and pulled my sleeve up as softly as he could. He cleared his throat like he was trying to reign himself in and repeated the process with the other arm.

"When?" he demanded.

"Saturday."

"Why?"

"Because I couldn't keep my big mouth shut. I shouldn't have said anything. But she basically said that I spent all of my money on myself. But I didn't. I barely spend anything on myself." I was rambling.

"Wrong. It's her fault. That's not how it's supposed to be. And for God's sake Jenna, stop hiding these things from me. I can handle it."

"I know you can, but I can't handle to see you angry like this."

He rubbed his raven short trimmed hair and blew out a breath.

"I'm not angry with you. You know that right? They just..."

"I know. I know. I won't hide it again. Ok?"

He nodded and we spent a few minutes in silence. He turned in his seat and was looking aggravated again.

"Go, Jenna, before I drive away, 'cause that's what I want to do. I want to drive away and not bring you back."

It somehow always shocked me how he wanted me with him and wanted to protect me all the time. I had never known someone who wanted to be with me and around me because they wanted to. The only people I knew wanted me around for what I could give them, or do for them and if I didn't, they didn't want me around. Even though it was still shocking, I was done questioning it.

"I love you. And it's as hard for me to go as it is for you to let go."

He put those warm, hardened-by- hard work hands on either side of my face and locked eyes with mine.

"You have no idea how much I love you, too. Tomorrow is Friday, so we have three days."

"Yeah, I'm gonna call you later ok?"

"You better." He was smiling again and it was easier to leave if he was smiling. Not easy, but easier.

I went home and was relieved that I was alone. I went to my room to change into some sneakers and retrieve my phone from under my mattress from where I hid it while it charged. There was a plug behind my bed so it was a perfect place.

I got it and turned it on. I put it in my bag and went to the kitchen to see if there was something to eat. There of course was nothing quick to make, so I left out early. I walked under the freeway and over two blocks to a Chinese place that sold $1 per entrée food. I walked in and ordered a portion of chicken lo mein and a drink. I saw down to eat it in one of the small booths.

I ate slowly, enjoying the peace. I looked at the clock and it was past time for me to go. I threw my trash in the can on my way out and pulled my phone from my purse.

He answered quickly and it startled me.

"Hello?"

"Hey, I'm walking to work."

"I've been waiting for you to call. They just called me in to work. They are giving me some overtime. I got some this weekend too. But I didn't want to miss your call. I'm in the car now, on my way."

"Hey, don't talk on the phone and drive. I'm glad I got to talk to you but drive and be careful, ok?"

"OK, I will. I'll see you tomorrow baby."

"Yeah, I'll see you tomorrow. Sunday..."

He sighed a heavy sigh... "Yeah Sunday. Bye"

I hung up first. I really didn't want him driving and talking on the phone.

I had to walk/run to work so I wouldn't be late.

I walked in and took up my usual duties. It was a not busy at all so the store was really quiet. I went to put the ordered sheet music in the store room when Mr. Cannon stopped me.

"Hey there, Little Lady, I just wanted to tell you that you've been doing a really good job and you're a Senior right?"

"Thank you and yes, I graduate in a month."

"Well congratulations and there might be something extra in your paycheck for a job well done and maybe a graduation gift." He winked at me.

"Thank you, Sir."

You could tell that this whole conversation was uncomfortable for him. I think he had unbuttoned the cuff on his flannel shirt about 18 times during our 4 sentence conversation.

I tried to save him.

"Ok, well, I've got to get going on these. Thanks again."

"No problem Little Lady, you get to work."

I shuffled and stacked sheet music for the next two hours. I went to retrieve my bag and made my way out of the store. I took my time walking the distance home. I wished Carlos wasn't working so I could call him but at the same time I was proud of him. He was really just a hard working, nice, guy and it was amazing that he loved me.

I got home and there was still nobody home. I washed some of May's new clothes that she had worn and then thrown on the floor. She now had three new pairs of shoes and I was grateful that they at least were buying her stuff in addition to themselves. It gave me some relief because soon, I was not going to be here to take care of her. The thought scared me and made me depressed, but I had to live my own life and staying and taking care of her would simply be enabling her.

I took a shower and put some mousse in my hair to make sure it was extra curly for tomorrow. I put on my favorite black pajama bottoms with the white stars and an old, grey, worn thin Batman t-shirt. I was hungry, but there was nothing in the house that didn't require defrosting or de-canning.

I decided to walk outside for a while and it cleared my head a little. By the time I made it back inside I was ready to go to bed. The house was still empty and I wondered if they had gotten a sitter for May or they were just keeping her out at all times of the night. She didn't have preschool on Fridays anyway, so I guess it was no big deal.

I crawled into bed after plugging my phone back in and read until I fell asleep.

Chapter 17

The next morning I checked for May but there was no one in the house. I got dressed and went to school. I walked to my locker. I came up the stairs and there he was in all of his glory. He was wearing the outfit I saw him in the very first time and he was smiling at me already, but he looked exhausted again as well. We collided in perfect unison and I relished in it. It was if his embrace refilled my tank. I was running on fumes when I wasn't with him. Just sputtering along until I got to him.

We didn't say anything. I didn't have any words and they were not necessary right now. He was at a loss to because he didn't utter a word as we stood together in the hall and let the world go on around us. But it seemed like only seconds before the bell rang. He placed his forehead against mine and said, "two days." I nodded; it was the only thing I was capable of at the moment.

I went through my classes as usual. Most of the teachers weren't even teaching at this point as graduation was coming up and even if I skipped all of the finals, I still had good grades.

I was making my way to third period when Carlos caught my elbow and pulled me to the side of the crowd. I barely made it without being mauled.

"Hey, I'm gonna leave. But I didn't want to go without telling you."

"Where are you going?" It was the middle of school for crying out loud.

"Work called on my cell. A guy got hurt today and they need a fill in and I could use the overtime."

"During school? They know you go to school right?" I thought it was ridiculous.

"Yeah, but I'm 18 and even if I skip my grades won't suffer. I need the money, J."

I mocked him by sticking my bottom lip out.

He ran his thumb over my lip and sighed like it hurt him.

"Don't you do that. Two days right? Two days and I get you all to myself."

I groaned.

"Ok, go to work. Sunday at noon, right?"

He smiled and it reached his eyes. "Oh, I knew you'd give in. Yes, noon."

"Just go." I smiled to let him know that I was joking.

"OK, bye." He pecked me on the forehead and was out of the hall before I knew it.

I whispered to no one, but me, "Two days"

I made it through the rest of the day and even though my Mom insisted on going, I was actually looking forward to shopping for my dress stuff tomorrow.

I got home and everyone was going about their business. And apparently a food run had been made because there was a full scale meal made and the remains of it were on the stove and the counter.

They were eating at the table and I thought I could get away with going to my room in peace. I was wrong.

"Jenna, I assume we're going tomorrow in the late afternoon since you have to go to your little job, right?"

I rolled my eyes to her referral to my 'little' job.

"Yeah, I get off *work* at noon, so we can leave about one, is that ok?"

"Yeah..." She crooned. "How exciting."

I went to my room and did my homework. Later in the middle of the night I snuck into the kitchen and ate some of the leftovers. When my Mom cooked it was really good food. I'd have to give her that.

I woke up at the butt crack of dawn the next morning and went to work. I worked until about eleven forty-five and went to ask Mr. Cannon if he had my check since I didn't work yesterday.

He was in the back office. It wasn't finished and the plywood walls were littered with calendars and receipts and pictures with funny sayings.

I knocked on the door jamb since there was no real door to knock on.

"Mr. Cannon?"

He turned around and the way he smiled reminded me of Santa Claus. Plus he was wearing a red flannel shirt with red suspenders and it just helped the image even more.

"There you are Little Lady. I was hoping you would stop by before you left for the day. I've got your check and something else for you."

"Sir? What else?"

"Just look in the envelope." He chuckled and it was certainly a belly full of jelly.

I opened the envelope and my regular paycheck was in it.

He said, "Here, sign it and I'll cash it for you."

"Thank you" I signed I and he went about counting out the right amount.

He handed it to me and said, "Go on...there's another one in there."

I made a questioning face and he just shooed his hands at me as if to make me hurry up.

I looked in the envelope and pulled out a wad of cash.

My eyes widened and my mouth opened and stayed that way.

Mr. Cannon smiled and said, "For your hard work. You deserve it."

It was all in twenty dollar bills but as I mentally counted, it was three hundred dollars.

I looked to Mr. Cannon and started to protest, but not too much.

He interrupted me. "Just close your mouth and say thank you."

I ran to him and hugged him as he chuckled and I must've said 'thank you' about two hundred times before I left.

I strolled home and before I reached the house I put the three hundred dollars in my bra. It was kinda weird, but there was really no safe place in my house to stash it. I felt like one of those old ladies in the grocery store who pulls out all of those sweaty bills out of her amply filled brazier. I shuddered in memory of it.

I walked into the house through the side door and brought my bag with me into the bedroom. I was so anxious about going to pick the fabric for my dress, mostly because I was excited and the rest was because my mom had insisted on coming with. I changed my shirt because after I had dusted a trumpet and climbed down the ladder, well, by the time I got down my shirt was covered in musical dust.

I changed into a fitted v-neck white t-shirt and left the jeans I had on. I was wearing my flip flops in case I had to try on shoes. I didn't know if we were shopping for shoes or not, but I wanted to be prepared.

I grabbed my bag and went back into the living room where my Mom sat on the couch. She looked like she was trying too hard. She had one of her new outfits on complete with these big gaudy red hoops that matched her stop light red shirt.

She looked disgusted when she said, "Jenna, is *that* what you're wearing?"

I looked down at myself and shrugged. "Yep."

"You could at least try not to embarrass me. I can't even imagine what kind of dress you're going to want."

Just then there was a knock at the door and Rebecca was standing outside clapping again.

I opened the door and stepped out before she could step in.

"Hi! Thank you again for doing this."

She was smiling and doing some kind of jig. "I'm so excited. Where's your Mom, let's go."

She appeared behind me, I could smell her. She smelled like she had bathed in department store perfume.

Rebecca motioned to her car which was a cross between a station wagon and an SUV and said, "Come on, let's go. We can take my car."

When we got to the car, Rebecca had gotten into the driver's side and unlocked the doors. My mom pushed me out of the way so she could sit in the front seat. It was childish and ridiculous.

We rode in silence most of the way and then Rebecca turned off of the freeway at an exit marked Downtown Los Angeles. I noticed the change of scenery and it was overwhelming. Stores were packed together and there was signage in every imaginable language. Some had shoes, some had purses, some had boots, and there were warehouses which advertised that they had any kind of fabric one would ever want.

Rebecca parked in a paid parking lot and got a ticket from the dispenser as she drove into it. We parked quickly and she got out and her whole demeanor had changed. She was like a woman on a mission and you could tell that this was her element.

"This way, come on." She sounded like a tour guide and put her arm through mine and completely ignored my Mom as we took off in a fast pace.

"Ok, Jenna, first we are going into a store to see what kind of style you want. I was going to get you some magazine pictures but I figured this was better."

Mom was barely keeping up and I snickered into my fist.

We headed into the first store after about three blocks of walking. I didn't think my mom was going to make it and she slumped into the first chair available. The store almost reminded me of a dry cleaner's. There were revolving racks everywhere and then I looked up and there were thousands of dresses hanging in bags.

I looked to Rebecca in awe and she was smiling like a Cheshire cat.

"Where do we start?" I asked her.

She grabbed my hand and towed me to the back. "Here."

We looked for an hour and I found a perfect dress. It was a beautiful shade of red that wasn't too bright but wasn't too dark. It was a halter top but the way it was cut didn't reveal too much cleavage. It was slit up the side, but it was a little too high for my taste.

I put the hanger around my neck and twirled around.

Rebecca was excited about it and said the shape would be flattering for my body shape and the color was perfect for my fair skin. I didn't know about that, but I knew I loved this dress and I loved the color. She also said that she could fix the slit so that it wasn't so revealing.

"Should we show it to your Mom?" She acted like she wasn't sure.

"Yeah, I guess. I mean, that's why she came, right?" I shrugged and started towards the front of the store.

We walked through the maze of dresses again and I stopped in front of my mom with a genuine smile.

She looked at the dress and up and me and back at the dress.

She flicked her finger, outlining the dress like she was drawing in the air.

"*This* is what you chose?" She said and her words were interwoven with disdain.

"Yes, isn't it gorgeous?"

She nodded and for a split second she had me fooled.

"Yes, it's perfect for a prostitute or a whorehouse. If that's the direction you're going then 'yes' it's perfect."

The most ironic part of her whole premise was that she was wearing a shirt and huge hoop earrings that were almost the exact same color.

I was absolutely humiliated. I had never been so ashamed of whom I was and the fact that she was my mother in my whole life. I had been to food banks, welfare offices, bought groceries in front of people from school with food stamps and everything in between. This was an all time low for me and being in her presence presently made me nauseated.

I had to do something before I puked.

I put the dress gently on the 'return' rack and walked back in front of Rebecca. "I think I'm done shopping Rebecca, but thanks. If you wouldn't mind, could you please just pick the fabric and make me whatever dress you think would suit me?"

Rebecca was still dumbfounded and her eyes, though her body was facing me, were still glued to my mother, unbelieving.

She grabbed my arm again and we went only three stores down and what looked from the outside to be a small store turned out to be the storefront for a huge fabric warehouse. She pulled me with her as she picked the most beautiful shimmery pale blue fabric. She said it was the perfect kind of fabric for the dress she had in mind.

I stood with her as the attendant cut the appropriate amount and handed it to us and pointed to the register. We went to the register and after showing her wholesale license I only ended up paying $60 in total for the fabric, thread and a zipper.

We made our way back to the store front and Rebecca held the bag all the way back to the car. It seemed as if she was as pissed as I was and I think she was a bit embarrassed for me. Hell, I wanted to hide under a rock.

We got into the car and my Mom started complaining that she was hungry and she wanted to stop and get something to eat. Rebecca pulled off of the freeway at our exit and proceeded to the nearest In & Out. My mom ordered enough food for her, Wallace and May. I didn't order anything and neither did Rebecca. When we pulled up to the first window my Mom feigned surprise at the fact that she had no cash. Then she tried some card and it was declined. Embarrassment apparently wanted to be my best friend today. I pulled out enough cash and handed it to Rebecca and then she handed me the change back.

We made our way home and as we were getting out Rebecca stopped me.

"Jenna, I really need to go ahead and take your measurements while you are here so I can get your dress done in enough time to make alterations if we need to. Why don't you come in and do it now?"

I was grateful for what she was doing and I started back to her house with her. My Mom started to follow us and Rebecca turned on her and was none too nice about it.

"Um...Miranda? I stopped because you said you were starving. Certainly Jenna can get her measurements taken by herself, right? I mean she is an adult. Why don't you go back to your house and eat and Jenna will be home shortly."

My Mom huffed but turned around nonetheless and made her way back home.

I followed Rebecca upstairs to this beautiful loft type room with a bay window. It had dress forms in every corner and fabric was splattered along the furniture like paint.

She said, "Ok, strip down to your skivvies and let's get your measurements."

I blushed and my mouth went slack.

She turned around and I was still dressed.

She snorted, "Oh Jenna, I'm sorry, all of my actors know to just strip and it's no big deal. Sorry honey. But really I've seen it all and you don't have to be shy around me, ok?"

My blush never left but I took off my shirt and jeans and stood before her almost naked and itching to put my clothes back on. She measured everything and then she asked me to put my arms up to measure my bust. She put the tape around my breasts and felt the bulge of money. I laughed and pulled it out and she gasped.

"Jenna, what are we old women?" She was giggling so hard.

"No, we are women who don't like our money stolen and who have no other place to hide it."

She shook her head and continued measuring. She finally finished up and wrote everything down and told me it was ok to put my clothes back on. I did so as quickly as I could and stuffed my money back into my bra as she giggled at me some more.

She asked me to sit down and I had to move some fabric before I could find a spot in the chair she pointed to.

"Jenna, I live here alone and I spend a lot of time up here. I see a lot through those windows."

"Oooook" I thought she was going to tell me all of the horrendous things my parents did when I wasn't around.

"I've seen that boy with you. I should say young man because I've seen the way he treats you in gesture and the way he handles you when you're upset. I don't want you to think that I've been spying, but sometimes I just see things. And let me tell you, that young man is in so deep, he couldn't get out if he tried."

I raised my eyebrows. "Deep?"

"Deep in love with you like I've never seen. He watches you like a hawk and treats you as if you are a creature to be worshipped. I've only seen you together about three times but you can't miss it. He's got it bad."

"You think?" I giggled.

"Yeah, and don't give him a hard time about it because honey, you're no better than him."

I blushed and giggled. "Yeah, I've got it bad too."

Her face got really solemn and she came and sat on a frumpy stool in front of me and grabbed my hands and said "Then you better get away from them and I'm not talking about down the street either. They're gonna ruin it. Trust me. Don't let them ruin that kind of love. You'll end up alone looking through windows while you sew." She squeezed my hands one more time.

There were tears welled up in her eyes and I felt her pain coming through her hands. I nodded and she got up and blew her nose on a nearby tissue.

"Thank you again, Rebecca, for everything."

She didn't turn towards me but said, "I'll probably have your dress ready within the week. I'll come get you for some alterations. You'd better get home before they punish you some more."

She turned her face to me, looking over her shoulder and winked.

I smiled at her and turned to go.

Chapter 18

I went home and went straight to my room. I didn't even want to look at my Mom's face anymore. She had humiliated me beyond reproach when we were shopping. And why would she ever think that I was even close to a slut or a whore or whatever she said? I had never even gotten that close to someone where I would consider that kind of intimacy, much less giving it out all over town.

I got into my pajamas and May and I had a very intense game of go fish in the closet. She had a new pair of pajamas on and I asked her where she got them.

"Mom said don't tell." She said it plainly and I'd never known her to lie.

"Why?" I pretended not to care.

She just shrugged and asked me if I had a Jack. I didn't and she had to go fish again. She groaned and then squealed a little squeal because she got a Jack when she went fishing.

We finished the game and I convinced her to brush her teeth. I went and did the same and washed my face. I reached under the cabinet for a towel to dry my face and there was so much stuff under the counter that I could barely reach the towels. I squatted down to look and it was shocking. There was new everything. There was new shampoo, soap, towels and everything. I couldn't believe my eyes. Everything was new and most of it still had the wrappers on or had never been opened.

Where are they getting all of this money?

I went to bed and woke up about 10 the next morning. When I woke up I took a shower, using my own stuff. I didn't even want to touch the stuff that they had bought until I knew exactly where it had come from. It just felt....off.

I got dressed in a tight pink scoop neck t-shirt and packed my sweater just in case, since he didn't tell me where we were going. I wore my favorite jeans and wore my hair down. I sprayed on some peach/cherry blossom body spray and put on some minimal make-up. I packed my sweater into my bag and walked out ready to go.

My Mom was up and was rooting around her special closet where she hid her bills and pills and God only knows what else. I walked through the living room to get a glass of water and she looked up at me.

"Where do you think you're going?" she sneered.

"Carlos is picking me up in a few minutes," I said back to her.

"You just couldn't wait, huh? So desperate to see him. Just desperate."

I didn't respond because at this point I just didn't care.

There was a knock on the door about the same time she opened her mouth to say something.

I grabbed my bag and headed to the door.

She had to move all of her stuff in a hurry because the closet door blocked the front door. She was taking a long time on purpose. It was petty, but I guess it was how she got her kicks.

As she was herding all of her stuff into the closet, I noticed a very familiar envelope sticking out but as soon as I did she stuffed it in along with the other piles and piles of envelopes. It was my cap and gown order. She had gotten it out of the mailbox? I just closed my eyes and let it mentally pile up with the other crap she had done to me.

I opened the door and stepped out. I went to close it behind me and Mom was there glaring at Carlos.

He didn't miss a beat.

"I wanted to apologize for getting Jenna here late last time. It won't happen again."

She didn't say a word to him. She just slammed the door and the wind from it blew my hair.

He grabbed my hand and led me towards his car opening my door first, of course.

I got a hunch and looked up into Rebecca's window as I got in and saw here there in her big bay window all by herself smiling at me. I waved to her and she waved back and then moved away from the window.

Carlos didn't say anything as he checked his side mirrors and then pulled onto the road. I turned towards him and smiled. I'd waited so long for this; the last two weeks had been hell.

I reached out and rubbed the back of his neck and he smiled at me.

"Where are we going? I didn't know how to dress," I asked.

"It's a surprise and you always look beautiful," he said.

When we got to the first stop light he turned in the opposite direction of the Pier, the movies, the mall and everything else I knew to do.

We kept driving for about twenty minutes and he made several turns and all I could see were apartment buildings.

Then he turned into a complex of buildings and parked.

Oh, tell me this is his apartment.

He smiled and came around to open my door. He was practically bouncing and I wondered what he was up to. Scratch that, I didn't care. We were together.

We walked up a set of stairs and came to a door marked 7A.

He pulled out his keys and unlocked the door. He opened it and let me in first. He took my bag from me and put it on the small brown leather couch. It was clean as a pin and there was something cooking or that had been cooked that smelled fantastic and my mouth watered.

He looked at me and I put my hands in the air silently speaking "Where are we?"

"This is my apartment. Saul is gone to the desert for the weekend with his friends. He won't be back until about 8 tonight. At least, he better not."

"It's great. Thank you for bringing me here. Can I look around?"

"Yeah, of course, J. Consider it yours."

I smiled at that thought and walked through to the kitchen and it was so clean, the counters gleamed. There were pots on the stove.

"You can cook?" I was surprised.

"Yeah, either you cook around here or you starve. Saul can't even scramble eggs."

We laughed and I walked away, wanting to explore the rest of his apartment. He walked behind me and I walked into a bedroom and turned around.

"Yours?"

He chuckled at that. "Yeah, how'd you know?"

I shrugged and then answered. "I don't know; it just seems like you."

I turned back and his room was as pristine as the rest of the house. He had a chocolate brown comforter on a double bed, but other than that his belongings were sparse. Either that or it was all put away.

He came behind me and rested his chin on my shoulder and wrapped his arms around my waist.

His chin bobbed on my shoulder as he spoke, "Are you hungry?"

"Yeah, I didn't eat today. I can't believe you cooked for me. Thank you."

"You're welcome. I hope you like chicken and rice. I didn't know what to make you."

He cooked for me when there were times that my own mother wouldn't cook for me and he did it out of love and not obligation. I couldn't contain myself any longer.

I turned around to face him. I was tearing up and he almost started talking, probably to ask me why I was crying. But I stopped him with my lips against his. It felt like his kiss was something I had been deprived of for years. I was starved for the taste of him and the heat of his mouth on mine. He gripped the back of my shirt right at the small of my back and pressed me against him. I rose up on my toes the slightest bit to make our mouths meet perfectly. My arms rose around his neck and my hands rubbed against that skull trimmed black hair. By instinct alone we turned our heads the tiniest bit to deepen what we had already started. I opened my mouth a small amount and he skillfully used it to his advantage. We continued this way until one mouth could not be distinguished from the other and just when I thought I would never get enough of him, my stomach grumbled.

We broke away slowly, revving down until we had both gotten a hold on our breaths and our want. The right side of my face was pressed against the right side of his face and I could tell by his breathing and the heaving of his chest that he was still trying to get control of himself. His strong arms were still wrapped around me and I could feel his muscles move as he drew patterns in my back with his fingers. It was unimaginable that I could make him feel this way.

He moved his hands slowly towards my hips. He quickly squeezed his hands on either side of them and said,

"That was..."

I smiled and said, "Yeah, it was..."

"Come on, I wanna see how you kiss me after you taste my cooking."

"Ok, let's see." I joked with him and we walked back to the kitchen area. He patted the stool by the bar in a gesture for me to sit.

"I can help. Don't make me sit here and not help."

He looked at me and frowned. "Jenna, when's the last time someone served you a meal?"

I looked down and just didn't want to answer. I had hardly ever been served dinner by anyone unless they were paid to wait on me.

He dropped the spoon into the pot and put the plate on the counter. He was next to me in a heartbeat. He coaxed me into facing him and put his arms around me.

"I'm sorry, baby. I'm sorry. I just want to do something for you today. I wanted to cook for you and just let you be free today."

I exhaled and let it all go. I would not spend this time worrying over people who didn't give a crap about me. Not anymore.

"It's fine. Thank you." I squeezed him around the middle and he kissed my hairline.

He went back towards the oven and pulled a cookie sheet out which had hot rolls on it. As he brought the pan up to place it on the stove I noticed his biceps and how the muscles around his neck flexed with the action. It was a sight to behold. He went back and resumed fixing a plate of chicken and rice and salad that was enough to feed a small army.

He pre-empted my argument by saying, "Just eat what you want. Don't worry about it."

I put one bite in my mouth and it was so delicious that I groaned out loud. Then I started giggling at his face.

"What?" I said, "It's amazing. I don't think I've ever had chicken and rice like this. I mean...damn."

He laughed and put his plate across from me and pulled a stool around to sit on.

"Well, if it causes you to make that sound every time you eat it, I'm gonna be making chicken and rice a lot."

I blushed, but never stopped eating because it was so good.

He got up and pulled two cans of Coke out of the fridge and gave me one.

I must've been hungrier than I thought because I ate most of what he served me. He finished his meal about the same time and banished me to the couch to wait for him to do the dishes.

"Can I turn on the TV or a movie or something?" I asked from the living room.

He leaned over the counter that we had eaten on and said "Jenna, this is your home, too. Do what you want to."

I sunk back into the couch and just sat there digesting my food and the words he had just spoken to me. That blue house wasn't my home and neither was this apartment. It was him and his embrace where I found home. No matter where we were, we were home when we were together. I sat there smiling for God knows how long.

I was still sitting there like a moron when he came into the living room. He looked at the TV and then back to me. As usual, he let me be. He didn't say anything about the TV not being on or ask me what I was doing.

"You wanna watch a movie?" He offered.

"Yeah," I shook myself out of my deep thoughts and got back to being present. "Whatcha got? We need something funny."

He pulled out these upright cabinets from either side of the entertainment center and rubbed his hands together. "Funny, funny, funny...Ok, we got Anchorman, Step-Brothers, Billy Madison..."

"Jeez, that's a lot of movies." He had probably hundreds of movies.

"Um...The Ballad of Ricky Bobby, Waterboy..."

I squealed and said "Waterboy, that's my favorite movie ever!"

He smiled and said "Ok, Waterboy it is."

He set up the DVD and TV then came to sit next to me, but he was a little too far away for my liking. As the movie began, he got back up and turned off all of the lights. He leaned back against the other side of the couch. He put one leg against the back of the couch and the other on the floor. He opened his arms and motioned me to get closer. I turned my back to him while I scooted back against his chest. After I got comfortable, he wrapped his arms around my waist and put his other leg against mine. My whole torso rose and fell with his breaths and he arms were warm against my waist and around my stomach. I traced the lines of his forearms lazily as we watched. We were mesmerized by the movie and when he laughed at Bobby Boucher I felt the rumbling against my back and it made me laugh harder.

I couldn't help myself and I quoted Bobby Boucher by heart: "I like school and I like football and I'm gonna keep doing them both..."

I refrained from quoting the rest of that scene to avoid a head on collision with my blush.

We finished the movie and he got up to turn the lights back on.

"Hey, I want to show you something." He said.

"OK." I got up and stretched. I reached up to the sky and flexed back and forth. When I finished stretching he was mid stride and staring at me. When he knew he was caught he cleared his throat, looked down at the floor and blushed.

"I saw that," I teased him.

"Yeah, I know. Let's go to the bedroom. I wanna show you something."

"Oh, really?" I joked.

"Oh, wow...who's the gutter brain now? Come on."

He led me by the hand to his bedroom and I waited, leaning against the door jamb while he opened the bottom drawer of his dresser and pulled put a small wooden box. He walked over to the bed and dumped it out. He jumped up on the bed and nodded his head towards the bed. I approached it and took off my flip flops before I got onto the bed. He gave me his hand to help me up and I sat next to him.

He picked up the first picture to show it to me. It was of two little boys. Carlos was sitting on the front of a red metal tricycle and there was a little boy behind him who I assumed was Saul.

I cooed as if the toddlers were in front of me. "Awww, that's so cute, look at your hair and your little shorts."

He looked at the picture and rubbed his head at the same time.

"Yeah, that's before I discovered how cool this cut is in the summer."

He showed me pictures of all of his family and said that his Dad wanted to meet me. He also mentioned that his brother was coming back at eight. I wondered if he wanted to meet me too.

We perused all of the pictures and I went through the ones of him as a child another round. I couldn't resist, they were so darned cute. I picked up the picture of him as a baby and the next thought in my head was whether or not our kids were going to be that gorgeous one day.

He put his arm around my waist and while I was still holding the picture he pulled me towards him and onto his lap. I was sitting sideways on his lap and he had his arms wrapped all the way around me and I put my head on his chest.

"Tell me what you're thinking when you look so serious."

He was haphazardly rubbing my arm while he waited for my answer.

I let out a breath and told him the truth, though I couldn't look at him while I said it.

"I was just wondering...you know...if one day our kids would look like this."

He tensed underneath me and I started backtracking.

"I'm sorry; you asked what I was thinking about...ughhh...sorry."

He took the picture from my hands and put them with the rest.

This is it. You've spilled your guts and it was too much too soon. What were you thinking? And if you were, did you have to say it? Idiot.

He moved and hooked his forefinger under my chin to make me look at him.

"Look at me, J."

I huffed out a breath that I had been holding and looked at him.

I figured I'd better meet this face on, so I scooted around so that I was facing him, still in his lap.

I looked up at him and what I expected to see wasn't there. When was I going to learn?

He moved his arms to go around my waist.

"You were thinking about our kids?" he asked me like he didn't believe me.

"Yeah, I just thought, you were such a beautiful baby and well, look at you now..." He half smiled at that. "I'm sorry, the thought just popped into my head."

"You think you're the only one? You don't think that I want a little brown haired Jenna toddling around?"

I looked at him questioningly and then a smile slowly crept across my face as I came to my senses once again and stopped doubting him, doubting us.

I was talking only in a whisper now. "You have?"

"Yes, Jenna. I want you for the rest of my life. I want *us* to be the family you deserved and never had. You *are* my family now."

His lips found mine and it was a new experience this time. It wasn't rushed or raw. Don't get me wrong it was sizzling. But this kiss was slower, deeper, and it carried all the words we meant, but didn't say tonight. It carried our past and solidified our future...together.

He grabbed me tighter and pressed our chests together but it didn't feel close enough. I moaned into his mouth and I couldn't believe I was making those noises.

He broke free and laughed, "That's the chicken and rice moan."

I laughed and hid my face in his neck because I was so embarrassed.

"You're gonna have to rename it. It sounds so lame." I laughed.

"It's the way you moan for me," he whispered into my ear.

I nodded, still hiding. "Yes, it is."

"Come on let's get off of this bed before I rethink this whole 'wait until you graduate to sweep you away' thing.

"Ok," I agreed and we picked up all of the photos and I cooed one more time at his baby photo before I placed it into the box.

"Hey, can you do me a favor?" I knew he would.

"Name it."

"You're gonna think I'm so weird."

"Spill it."

I reached into my shirt and he reddened.

"What kind of favor are we talking about here? I take it back."

I pulled out my bonus money and showed it to him.

"This is the bonus I got at work today. It was in...you know...there...because I can't hide it at home."

"Because they'll take it again..."

"Yup."

He was kneeling on the ground putting his box of pictures in his drawer.

"You want me to keep it for you?"

"Yeah, if that's ok."

"Of course it is. Here." He took the money from me and pulled out his wallet. It had a space for cash and he had some in it and it had another space for cash that was empty. He put my money in it and said. "There. You've got a space in my home, my heart and now my wallet."

I rolled my eyes at his cheesiness.

We walked into the living room and sat down on the couch. I turned and put my feet on his lap and he didn't move them, he started rubbing my feet for me. He turned on some Credence Clearwater Revival with a remote. I loved the classic rock stuff just like he did and we talked for a while going back and forth about bands.

He got a mischievous look on his face and said, "Tell me about prom dress shopping."

"Ugh...it was humiliating."

He tried to stifle his laughter but it wasn't working.

"I thought it was supposed to be fun."

I was enjoying his hands on me a little too much to be talking about bad things, but I continued telling him the story.

"It was fine until I showed Mom the dress I wanted and she..."

He stopped rubbing my feet and changed the tone of his voice.

"What'd she say or do?"

"See? You're getting pissed off. Nope, I'm not telling you. I don't want to spend our time like that."

He put his head back and looked at the ceiling.

"I won't be pissed. Ok, ok, I will *try* not to be pissed. Tell me."

I groaned. I knew it wasn't me he was angry with but I still didn't like it.

"Fine. She said that the dress and the color I picked out was a perfect choice for prostitutes and whorehouses."

I looked up at the ceiling like he had done before and forbade myself to cry.

He let me stay that way for a few minutes and then wiggled one of my feet to get my attention.

"Hey, come here."

I hesitated because I was still composing myself. But I couldn't resist him or the comfort I felt from his presence.

I looked over at him and he reached over and pulled me over to him and engulfed me in his embrace. He didn't say anything. He didn't have to. I knew that the way my mother acted affected him now as much as it did me.

While he was still holding me I finished the story and told him all about Rebecca and what she had said about us.

"She's right."

"Yeah, I'm in pretty deep over here," I admitted.

"She was right about me too." I hugged him tighter and replied, "I know."

We stayed like that until the lock on the door jiggled a bit and scared the crap out of me.

"It's just my brother. He has the damndest time with that lock. It's funny to watch him struggle with it for a few minutes though."

"You are a shame. Go help him."

He moved to get up and just as he did, his brother won the war with the lock and entered the apartment.

He walked in and put a bag and a helmet on the floor in the front hallway and smiled as he broached the living room.

He was a little taller than Carlos. His skin was a little darker than Carlos' too and he was skinnier than a stray cat.

He extended his hand, "Hey, I'm Saul. You must be Jenna."

I reached my arm out to shake his hand. "Yeah, I'm Jenna, nice to meet you."

He walked back to retrieve his bag and told Carlos, "I'm going...um...out tonight. Won't be back until tomorrow sometime."

Carlos just shrugged and replied, "Yeah, ok."

Saul went in his room and dumped all of his stuff out, packed it up again and was saying "Goodbye" before we knew it.

I looked at him and said, "Time?"

He checked his watch, "8:12, we've got two hours."

He was looking straight ahead and was desperately trying to hide a smile on his face.

"Ok, your turn. What are thinking about when you grin like that? Or do I want to know?"

"I was thinking about what I could bribe you with to make you tell me about your dress."

I was trying so hard to be a hard-ass about it. "Nothing." I crossed my arms over my chest.

"Ice-Cream?" *Damn you cold creamy treat.*

I didn't hesitate. "Done. Let's go."

I got up and grabbed my stuff and headed towards the door. He wasn't following me so I looked back and he was laughing so hard that he was doubled over.

"It's not that funny." I was putting on my mean girl face, which is so far from mean it's pitiful and squinted my eyes at him while tapping my foot in mock anger.

He got up and grabbed his keys and headed towards me.

He was trying to make himself stop laughing but it was in vain.

"You'd be a pitiful hostage. They'd just offer you ice cream and you'd tell them everything."

"True...but you love me, so it's ok."

His whole face became as serious as I've ever seen it.

"Remember that, J." He smiled again and swatted me on the butt and said "Now...ice cream for the woman."

I laughed at him and we left on a quest for my bribe.

We drove out to Ben & Jerry's and he had never been there before.

I looked at him like he was out of his mind.

I rushed to the counter and order my favorite cup of Phish Food. He was still looking and I offered him a bite of mine to try it.

"I don't like chocolate, Jenna." My whole face dropped and I nearly dropped my cup of ice cream.

"Now we have to break up." I tried to look like my world had fallen apart.

"I don't like peanut butter either." He shrugged as he said it.

I stuck my spoon into my ice cream violently and said, "That's it, take me home, we're sooo over."

He laughed and leaned into me so that the whole ice cream shop didn't hear him. "There's better things than chocolate and peanut butter, J."

I giggled, "Dirty....Go get some ice cream before you melt mine."

He laughed and ordered a scoop of Banana Split.

We decided to go sit at the beach and finish our ice cream. We still had a little over an hour before we needed to leave to get back *on time.* We parked in the parking lot by the Pier right on the edge between the parking lot and the beach. We both sat on the hood of his car.

I was thoroughly enjoying my Phish Food and watching the waves roll in and out. The moon was illuminating them and made them look unreal.

I felt him looking at me and stopped eating. "What?"

"You got your bribe, where's my details?"

"Well, the truth is that I don't know other than the color."

"I'll take it, what color."

"It's a light blue. That's the fabric we bought."

He nodded.

He resumed eating and finished it way before I did but waited until I finished before he walked over to throw them away.

We sat there together in silence and I looked at his watch way too often.

I just didn't want to make that mistake again.

"We've got time, plus I set my watch ten minutes faster."

I tried to be happy even though my stomach was turning somersaults because I had to go back home.

"You know what the best thing is about Sunday dates?"

"What?"

"You get to see me tomorrow."

"True. But you know what would be better?"

"What?"

"Saying 'let's go home' and meaning the same place."

I moved closer to him and we held each other until it was time to go home.

He dropped me off and I knew she was going to have something to say about me spending almost eleven hours with him. *She'll get over it. She can't control me forever.*

I walked in the door and she was getting laundry out of the dryer.

"Didn't know if you were coming home or not," she spat.

"I live here," I said it quietly.

"I didn't give you permission to stay out with a guy for twelve hours."

It was all I could do not to give her a smart remark about it only being eleven hours.

"I didn't ask, Mom. I didn't ask."

"If you live under this roof, you're not going to whore around with a guy for eleven hours at a time and call it a date."

"Mom, I'm not a whore. He's my first real boyfriend."

"Doesn't have to be to fit the bill. I remember being a teenager."

"Well, I'm not like you."

I walked into my room and changed into my pajamas. I went into the bathroom and brushed my teeth and said 'to hell' with the rest.

The rest of the week went fast and by Thursday I was over-ready for the weekend to be here. Rebecca had come over on Tuesday afternoon and wanted me at her house on Saturday afternoon to try the dress on and see what alterations needed to be done. My schedule had been changed at work so I now had to work Fridays instead of Thursdays, which was fine because Carlos worked Friday nights anyway, so it wasn't as if we could go anywhere.

I got to sixth period a little early and Carlos was already waiting for me in our spot in the corner.

I sat down and ran my hand down his back and said, "Hi."

He turned towards me in his desk and said, "Guess what?"

"What?"

"I'm taking you to dinner tonight."

"On a school night?" I fake gasped.

"Yep. Chinese?" He knew I loved Chinese.

"Yum. I should call my Mom so she doesn't have the excuse that I didn't tell her."

He rolled his eyes. "Ugh...Is it graduation yet so you can get out of there?"

"I wish."

I called my Mom and told her instead of my routine of asking her for permission. She gave me an earful of grief over it but I reminded her that I wasn't asking. She was positively livid and said, "Hope you have a good meal." Whatever that meant.

We went to eat and it was a nice change of pace to be out on a school night.

He dropped me off at home and I went to get out and he pulled me back into the car for one more kiss before I got out. I looked up and waved at Rebecca. She looked at me but didn't wave back.

I walked into the house and the place was a wreck. The cabinets were open again like one of those creepy ghost movies and the dishes were dirty. My stomach threw itself into knots at the sight and my imagination went wild at whom or what awaited me when I crossed the threshold into the rest of the house.

I heard, "Jenna, are you *finally* home?"

"Yes...I'm... in the kitchen." *I don't think Chinese is my favorite food anymore.*

"Did you have a good time?" she asked and not in a good way.

"Yes, we had fun." My brain was scrambling to figure out where this was going so I could shuffle around it.

"And was the food good? Where did you eat?"

I reached into the refrigerator to get something to drink but there was nothing so I closed it.

"Yeah, we went to eat Chinese. It was good. I've never been to that place before."

I looked back at her. Fake smile alert.

"Well, while you were traipsing around town filling up your fat gut we were sitting here hungry. May went to bed hungry."

"Why don't we have any food?" With all the shopping that's been going on certainly they could've hit up the grocery store.

"Because we don't have any money, stupid." She was getting closer to me and I stepped back, but I was against the refrigerator.

"Mom, y'all have been buying clothes and shoes and everything else for weeks. We have to have some kind of money." *I wanted to say 'Duh!'*

"That's none of your business. And they ran out, I mean, we ran out of money."

"Well, take back some of that stuff and get some food."

I was done with this conversation and so I moved forward to get around her.

It happened so fast I couldn't move or stop it. She reached out and slammed the right side of my head against the stove top. It hit one of the burners and I flopped onto my butt on the floor. My face nearly hit the refrigerator.

I reached up and my hand came back with blood. She crouched down and got into my face and I could smell her rancid breath. It was a mix of sewage and coffee and my beloved Chinese knocked at the door of my stomach wanting to be freed.

"You filthy fat bitch. You go out with your little bastard boyfriend and eat and be happy while the rest of us stay here and you have the gall to come home and tell me what to do. Don't you know the only reason he's treating you good now is so that he can make your life hell later? You think you'll have it any better than me?"

I wanted to scream at her. I wanted to push her backwards and watch her fall on her ass. But my vision was blurry and I was getting dizzy. I couldn't do anything but sit there like a loser.

And then it hit me as I looked into her face. It hit me harder than she ever had and summoned up feelings that I didn't want to feel for her. I felt sorry for her. I pitied her. All of this hatred and resentment towards me was jealousy, in the purest and simplest form.

She finally got out of my face and it took me 10 minutes to come to my senses. She was sitting at the kitchen table doing...something.

I reached into my bag and got my phone out. I called Carlos and he answered on the first ring.

"Are you ok?"

She saw me on the phone but didn't even flinch. She probably already knew I had it.

"No, can you come and get me?"

"What happened, Jenna?" his voice was virtually a roar. "I'm getting into my car now."

"Ok, I'm gonna get some ice. Just come to the side door."

"Ice? Jesus, OK, I'm coming."

I put down the phone. I scooted, still on the floor over to the floor and pulled a dishrag down from the side of the sink. She got up then and begrudgingly grabbed the rag from me and opened the freezer and filled it with ice and jabbed it towards me.

I put it on my head. I leaned up against the cabinets now behind me for I don't know how long.

I heard the screeching of tires and the side door flew open. He didn't even bother to knock.

He rushed to me and removed the dishtowel from my head and looked at it.

He got into a different position and lifted me up to standing and then reached under my legs and carried me out.

He turned around before he reached the threshold of the kitchen and was talking to my mother.

"What in the f- is wrong with you? She's your daughter."

She shot him the middle finger and I don't even know if he saw it.

Chapter 19

He brought me home begrudgingly as he really wanted to take me to the hospital. But the cut was superficial and I hated the smell of hospitals.

We went in and his brother was not there. I didn't know if it was me or if he just never stayed here. I walked straight to the couch and Carlos went to the kitchen for something. I just sat there. This, apparently, was a great couch for thinking.

He came back into the room with a new dishtowel with new ice in it and swapped mine out for the new one. He handed me 3 little oval shaped blue pills and a glass of water. I took them without saying anything.

I didn't deserve this guy that was running around rescuing me from my life. I wondered what he saw in me that made him think that it was all worth it. I looked at him and said,

"I need to wash the blood off. Can I use your bathroom?"

"Yeah. Leave the door unlocked in case you need me."

He was being distant. My heart told me it was because he was angry with my Mom. My brain told me he was realizing how 'not worth it' this whole thing really was.

"OK." I made my way to the bathroom and I looked like the ending scene of Carrie. There was blood down my face, down my shirt and even some on my shoes.

I must've gasped because he was in the bathroom next to me within seconds.

"What happened?" He looked alarmed

"Nothing. I scared the crap out of myself. Look at me."

Then I looked at him and he had blood on his clothes too.

I tried to joke and pointed to his shirt.

"Oh, I leaked on you too."

"You *should* be at the hospital but damned if I can make you do anything."

He was pissed. He got into the cabinet under the sink and pulled out hydrogen peroxide and cotton balls and some kind of ointment.

He motioned for me to sit on the counter and I did. He prepped the cotton balls with hydrogen peroxide and went to work.

"There's blood in your hair. You're gonna have to take a shower and wash it out."

"I don't have any clothes."

"You can wear something of mine."

I nodded and felt just awful for putting this burden on his life.

He finished up and came to stand in front of me between my legs, but I couldn't look him in the face yet.

I leaned forward and put my forehead in his chest and let his rising and falling chest calm me down.

"How mad are you?" I asked.

"I'm so pissed off that I could kill someone with my bare hands."

I thought he meant me. I knew better, but I still thought it. I always assumed that one of these days he was going to realize that this was my fault. If I stood up to them more. If I wasn't such a smart ass. If I could keep my mouth shut for 5 seconds.

"OK, you need to take a shower and get some sleep. The cut isn't that deep but it bled a lot so we need to keep an eye on you. Do you feel sick to your stomach?

I still had my forehead attached to his chest and I shook my head 'no' and could feel the front of my hair knotting up in his shirt.

"For the love of God, Jenna, look at me."

He got a head shake 'no' again.

He took three extremely long deep breaths and said, "Ok, towels are in the cabinet and while you are in there I will find you something to wear."

He moved away and I nearly keeled over the side of the counter head first. When he left he didn't close the door all the way.

I felt nasty and sticky and I wanted to just wash away everything that had just happened.

I got undressed and got into the shower. I turned it on as hot as it would go and watched the water turn 'black cherry Kool-aid' red underneath me and spin into the drain.

I tenderly washed my hair and the rest of myself got a scrub. It's amazing what hot shower can accomplish.

When I turned off the water a towel appeared over the top of the shower door. I took it and wrapped it around myself under my arms. I stepped out from the shower stall and he was leaned up against the counter with his arms crossed looking at the floor. It was reminiscent of how he stood against my locker. Even with everything that had happened, him standing there with his biceps bulging as his arms were folded was the sexiest image I had ever seen. My toes itched and squirmed in the bath mat underneath me in an attempt to run to him.

"Are you ok? Dizzy? Nauseated?" He was still looking down as he spoke to me.

"No, I'm feeling a lot better."

"I can't do this anymore," he whispered, and in the split second after he said it I thought me meant me...again, I underestimated him.

But then his body was pressed up against mine and he carefully backed me up into the shower stall and his right hand was between my shoulder blades and his left hand was roaming slowly south down my back. It didn't stop roaming until it found a resting place between the back of my thigh and my butt. And soon after, his left hand joined his right on the other side. He squeezed slightly and my entire body came alive.

I couldn't reach up because I would lose my towel so I let my arms surround his gorgeous torso and he was looking down at me like it was the first time he had seen me.

"I didn't know what was going to happen. I didn't know how hurt you were or in what condition I was going to find you. I almost lost it Jenna. What would I have done?" He was choking up as he said it and I swore I saw tears pooling in his eyes.

I didn't have time to answer. His lips captured mine and we were aligned from head to toe and pressed together so that there was not an inch of space between us.

I felt his mouth open slightly and I didn't wait for him this time. I matched his mouth with mine and our tongues met and we both moaned at the same time in bliss. This went on for only a few minutes and I could feel him slowing us down. He pulled back one final time and kissed my bottom lip and then my top lip.

"I need to get a shower too. And I need you to stay right here. I will only be 5 minutes." My eyes must have grown three times their regular size.

"Nope, don't give me those wide eyes. Turn around or hide your eyes or whatever, but please don't go anywhere."

He reached in and turned on the shower and I turned around quickly while he stepped in and started to put on the navy blue boxers and gray t shirt he put on the counter for me.

After a few minutes, I heard the water turn off and I threw a towel over the door as he had done for me.

He took it and I could hear the swishing of the towel as he dried off. He came out with it around his waist and I finally got a look at all of those tattoos. There was a cross over his chest and a dragon looking thing on his arm. He also had a spider web on his leg and two tribal looking stars on either side of his chest.

I swiped at my mouth to make sure that I wasn't drooling.

"Don't look at me like that when I'm standing here in just a towel. It's dangerous."

"For who? Me or you?" I put my hand on my hip and felt like I was ok again.

"There she is. My girl has come back."

He walked out of the bathroom and I heard him open a drawer and heard his towel drop. He was making me blush from the next room over. Boy's got talent.

He came back in and opened a drawer. It might've been my head, but that was the loudest drawer I'd ever heard. He pulled out a magenta toothbrush still in the package and opened it and handed it to me.

"You keep extra pink toothbrushes?"

"Not until recently. I've got this amazing girl, and I told her that she was my family now and that this was her home too, so I figured I'd better stock up."

We stood there and stared at each other through our reflections and he finally broke the stare and left, closing the door behind him.

I brushed my teeth and took a look at my head one more time and went into the bedroom. He was there picking up his towel and coming towards the bathroom.

"My turn." He smiled and shut the door behind him.

I heard the water running and being shut off and on and off again.

He came out and I was still standing in the same place.

He wrapped his bulky arms around me from behind and said, "It's ok, J, are you scared of sleeping?"

"Sleeping is not what's keeping me from that bed and you know it."

"Well, the sheets are clean. I can't think of anything else." He huffed out a laugh.

"Hmmm...well, only because you bought me a pink toothbrush."

"I bought three. I hoped that you'd be here often."

He went around me, turned off the light and got into the bed. He pulled back my side of the covers and waited.

He lay back and let me be, let me decide when I was ready.

I crawled in beside him and he turned towards me. And as if we'd laid together for years we both moved arms and legs where we were tangled together comfortably and the top of my head was underneath his chin. He reached down and pulled the covers over us and that was the last thing I remember.

Chapter 20

I woke up at who knows what time and stretched only to find that there was someone stretching behind me. His chest was on my back and one of his legs was thrown over top of mine. He moved my hair away from my neck and began a cross between kissing and nibbling his way along the back of my neck.

My head lay on his right bicep, it made a perfect pillow. And the other arm was draped around my waist and lay limp across my stomach.

He got closer to my ear and then his teeth ran along the edge of my earlobe as he said, "Good morning."

I smiled and stretched while turning around to face him. My hand came down and brushed my face as I released from my stretch and I winced. It was sore.

I nuzzled my face in his neck and whispered, "Good morning back to you."

As he barely touched my head he said, "How's your head?"

"Mmmmmm, it's been better."

"I always imagined you in my bed in the morning, but not quite like this."

I slapped his chest. "I'm not sure, but I think we missed school."

"I could give a flying flip about school right now."

I had pulled back from his neck and was tracing his cross tattoo with my finger.

He looked down to where my finger was and laughed.

"Oh, I forgot about your tattoo fetish."

"I don't have a fetish…it just makes you hotter."

"You think I'm hot?" He was barely whispering, his voice had gone so quiet.

"You know that it's all I can do to keep my hands off of you right?

He nodded a yes and took my face in his hands and said, "Sometimes I can't believe you walked into that class with me. And now you're in my bed telling me that you want me and I'm about to make you breakfast."

"Ooooh, yum, I'm starving."

"That's all you got out of what I said?" He laughed.

"Yup." I winked and rolled out of bed on the other side.

"Come sit in the kitchen while I cook for you."

"Only if you let me cook for you sometime."

"Deal." He pulled out eggs and pancake mix and started pulling bowls and utensils out like a pro. He made us breakfast and it didn't disappoint.

We finished eating and I looked down at my clothes.

"I need to go home and get some clothes."

He had his elbows on the counter and had put his head down and scrubbed his head with his hands. I could see from the side of his counter that he had started the knee bobbing thing again.

It was my turn to be the comforter and I took the opportunity.

I walked over to where he was and removed his hands from his head and pulled them towards me.

He turned and held onto me around my waist.

"Don't go home," he said it so desperately.

"I just want to go get some clothes right now. They're probably not even home. How long can I stay here?"

He fisted the sides of my...well his...t shirt and sounded so pained when he said, "I wish you would stop calling this place mine. Don't you know by now that anything that is mine is yours?"

"Ok, so can we go to *their* house and get me some clothes and come back *home*?"

That bucked him up quick and he was in the bedroom getting dressed before I knew it.

He came back through to the kitchen still pulling his shirt over his head. He was grinning almost as brightly as the night he asked me to marry him.

"Ready?" he said.

"Let me get dressed."

I put my jeans on from the night before. They had made it almost unscathed. I kept his t shirt on and remembered that I kept an extra pair of flip flops in my bag since my Chucks were maimed.

I walked out into the living room and he was cleaning up the kitchen.

"Is there any way you grabbed my purse? I know there were more important things but I was just wondering."

"Kinda. It was still attached to your arm when I picked you up."

He pointed towards the front door and I saw it.

"Now are you ready?" I asked.

"Not really, but I guess you can't walk around here naked. Wait..."

"Stop."

"Ok, ok, let's go."

We pulled up at my house and I thanked the Lord that they weren't home. I ran inside as fast as I could and grabbed a bag and stuffed random clothes in it. I didn't even know what I was packing. I ran to the bathroom and picked up some essentials and went back to my room to grab some books.

I saw that I was still in the clear when I came out of the house and Carlos was in front of Rebecca's house talking to him. They were nodding and talking as I walked over to them. He took my bag from me and Rebecca smiled. "Jenna, your dress is almost done. We can do some last minute alterations next Friday night instead of tonight. Sound good?"

"Yes. Thank you so much."

She smiled and started back towards her house. Carlos took my hand and we got back in the car.

"Do you need anything else? Do you need me to stop somewhere?"

"Nope, I'm good. What are the plans today?" I didn't know what we were going to do or how long I was staying with him.

"Well, I thought we'd stop at the grocery store and get some stuff for you to cook dinner if you're up for it."

"Yeah, you like spaghetti?

"Ugh...I love spaghetti. Here we are."

We went into the store and bought what we needed to make dinner. We had a small argument about who was going to pay when we got to the register. I lost.

We got home...home...and put the groceries away. I went to take another shower and changed my clothes. I was brushing out my hair when he came into the bathroom. He sat just watching me.

"What?" I asked. I was not that interesting.

"Just enjoying watching you do regular stuff." He smiled.

"Ooook."

"Can we talk?" He was hesitant

I tried not to miss a beat. But his tone made me nervous.

"Yeah." I barely spit it out.

"Are you going back there?

"I don't know. We only have one more week until prom and three weeks until graduation and then I go to see my Dad. What do you think?"

"What do I think? I think you should never go back again. I think you should never even speak to those people ever. I think...I think I don't want you to leave me here wondering if you're alive or not."

"I'm gonna have to go back sometime. I need to talk to May. I need to get my stuff. I need to tell them how awful they are...for me. I need to get that out. It has to be said."

And what I didn't say was that leaving like that felt like letting them win. It felt like I was weak. It felt like they had finally gotten what they wanted.

"I think I'm gonna stay here until Sunday and then go back." He winced at my words.

"I can't believe you would go back after everything." He got off of the counter and walked out.

I wanted to give him some space so I sat on the closed lid of the toilet and blubbered quietly. I cried until I couldn't cry anymore.

I felt like I was hurting him and that was the last thing I wanted to do. I got up and wiped my face and started putting stuff back into my bag. I would gladly go back to that house before I stayed here and hurt him anymore.

I brought my bag out to the living room and he was in the kitchen filling a pot with water. I guess he was going to start cooking. I put the bag on the couch and he turned with the pot and put it on the stove, but his eyes were on the bag.

He walked over to me while I was sitting on the couch putting my shoes on.

"Don't do this, Jenna." He sat on the coffee table right in front of me as I was tying my shoes.

"I have to. I'm here and I'm hurting you. I appreciate you coming to get me and helping me. But I can't do this to you. I know you don't understand and hell, neither do I, but I just feel like I need to go back and...I can't explain it...it just needs to be done."

"OK, I get it. But I thought you were leaving on Sunday."

"Why? So I can hurt you all weekend? So I can continue to see that look on your face? No thanks."

"Look at me." I was trying my best to be angry so it didn't hurt so badly.

"Jenna, please look at me." He was pleading and I couldn't resist no matter how hard I tried.

I looked up, but didn't say anything. We looked at each other for what seemed like forever. He must've seen my walls slowly back down because as I let go of my anger, he reached for me. He pulled me onto his lap and we held each other until I knew he understood. I wanted him and I wanted this, but letting them force me out didn't give me the closure I thought I needed.

He reached behind me and took my shoes off.

I laughed into his neck and he laughed back.

"I know you need to do whatever you need to do, Jenna, but give me until Sunday. Let me have you to myself until Sunday."

"Ok, I'm yours."

"Was that our first fight?"

"I don't know, but it sucked."

We made spaghetti together and spent the rest of the weekend in contented peace. I read while he watched TV, he called into work which worried me; we cooked and laughed and had fun. We were happy, if only for the weekend.

Carlos' home phone rang about nine on Saturday night. He answered it and he said 'hello' but didn't say anything for a while after. I finally looked over to him and he was looking at me and he looked...he looked pissed. I got up and went over to him and he put the phone to my ear momentarily. It was my mother and she was in full form.

She was screaming and cussing and calling him names and threatening everything from his job to his crotch to his health. She threatened to go to his boss and make him lose his job. She threatened to be at his apartment one day and kill him while he slept and then my step-Dad got on the phone. We were both sitting on the floor with the phone receiver bookended by our ears.

When he got on the phone it was like listening to him as he berated my mom. He threatened the same things as my mom did, but continued. He said he would bomb his entire apartment building. He said he would buy a gun and meet Carlos at school and kill him.

Why all of the sudden did they care? Why? I know by what my mom said the other night that she was jealous of what I had. But why him? And then it hit me the way her motives had hit me the other day. It was the loss of control that had thrown him over the edge. He was always controlling us. I really thought that half of the stuff Mom did to me was because he was prompting her to. He controlled everything in the house and now he was trying to exert his power over me too.

I spoke up and interrupted his tirade.

"Look, it's Jenna. I will come home tomorrow afternoon." Carlos looked at me like I had slapped him in the face. "I will come home then and not before. And one way or another I will be out of your house within the next three weeks."

"We'll see about that." With that he hung up. I didn't know if he meant about coming home tomorrow or if I'd be out in three weeks.

We sat on the floor for thirty minutes in silence.

He stood up and helped me up and we walked into the bathroom looking like zombies and brushed our teeth in silence.

We both got into the bed and we lay together, tangled up and torn.

I looked up at him and he looked at me with such sadness.

"Carlos," I whispered.

"Yeah."

"Just...just kiss me until I forget everything but you."

And he did.

Chapter 21

I went home the next day after the best weekend of my life, despite the bad stuff. I was determined not to let them hurt Carlos and I was also determined to finish high school without running away. The more I thought about what Rebecca had said to me, the more I knew what had to be done. Her words echoed to me:

"Then you better get away from them and I'm not talking about down the street either. They're gonna ruin it. Trust me. Don't let them ruin that kind of love. You'll end up alone looking through windows while you sew."

Like God was speaking to me, maybe He was; I had a plan. I will remember it for the rest of my life, the day I realized how I needed to play this. Lots of things would have to go right, but I could make it work. I got my stuff unpacked and washed all of my clothes.

May was staying away from me. I'm sure they had planted some crap in her head.

I went to bed scheming, but I couldn't tell Carlos or anyone else yet. There were other factors and parties involved and I didn't know if I would have their cooperation or not.

Carlos was still worried the next week but I assured him that they weren't even speaking to me and hadn't all week. It was just a play of power. He had been working tons but we were both looking forward to prom.

I went Friday night and tried on my prom dress at Rebecca's house. It fit perfectly and was long and had spaghetti straps and the cut up to the thigh. I suddenly panicked because I had forgotten to buy shoes. But Rebecca, thankfully, wore the same size that I did and loaned me the prettiest silver heels. She offered to do my hair for me and I thanked her. Mom hadn't said anything all week and she certainly was not even going to recognize that I was going to the prom.

Carlos was supposed to pick me up at eight. I went to work at the sheet music store until two.

I got home and took a shower and got my make-up bag and other stuff and headed to Rebecca's house. My mom saw me leaving and said, "Where are you going with all of that?"

"Rebecca offered to do my hair and is going to let me get dressed at her house so I don't bother...anybody."

I saw something in her that I hadn't seen in a while. It was regret. It was only a flash and then it was gone.

"Go ahead then, what are you waiting for?"

I went over to Rebecca's house and when I went in, boy was she ready for me.

She had every kind of beauty supply known to man and some I had no clue what they were. I was so scared.

She primped me and we giggled all day until about seven thirty when she sent me home looking like a princess wrapped in a cloud of blue.

I walked in and May ran to me, whether she was supposed to I didn't know. She made me show her my earrings which were also borrowed from Rebecca. I went and put all my things away, sprayed myself with perfume and packed a few necessities in my little silver purse, another borrowed accessory.

I went into my room and tried to fold some clothes just to be busy and out of sight. About fifteen minutes later, ten minutes early, Carlos knocked on the door and I nearly ran to get it.

My mom was there first, of course, and she just stared at me. She didn't say I looked pretty or anything. She stared like she was just opening the door for a roommate to walk through, nothing more than an acquaintance.

Before I reached the door I looked her dead in the eyes and said, "I'm not going to be back anywhere near eleven tonight. It's prom night." She didn't even blink. It was like looking at a stranger.

I stepped out of the door and Carlos was dumbfounded. I giggled a bit and all he could choke out was, "Damn." I was thinking the same thing because boy did he look good in a tux.

We walked to his car and drove to one more milestone until we could be together for good.

Prom was just a weird dance where everyone was kinda awkward. We danced some, we sat at weird decorated tables and we took pictures where the photographer left from behind the camera and adjusted our elbows and hands.

I was glad to be leaving. Carlos was starving and I laughed my butt off at him as he went through a drive in and ordered two Big Macs from McDonald's.

"Ok, where to next?" I asked as he finished off his last bite.

"Those after parties can get pretty rowdy. My brother went to some last year and he said he left after a few minutes. Let's go to the beach."

"In this? I pointed to my dress.

He put on a serious face and said, "No, you should take it off and run around the beach naked."

I narrowed my eyes at him and he laughed and put the car into gear and took off towards the beach.

We parked in our usual spot and it was apparent that we weren't the only ones who had the same idea.

"So, there are two things that I wanted to show you." He was taking off his tux jacket as he said it.

"Ok." This wasn't joking around. He meant business. I could see the lines in his face creasing.

"Let's go sit on the beach." He said. He was acting very suspicious.

"Ok"

We got out of the car and he laid out a blanket for us to sit on. I didn't know where in the heck it came from but it was thoughtful.

We sat there in silence for a while, watching the waves roll in and out.

He first pulled out a long black box and opened it in front of me. I couldn't believe he had bought something for me. As if his existence in my life wasn't enough. It was a bracelet made of little hearts: one gold, one silver and one rose gold and the pattern began again.

It was so delicate that I was afraid to touch it.

He took it out and put it on my wrist.

I reached out to kiss him. I wanted to jump over to his side of the blanket and thank him properly. But he stopped me.

I cocked my head sideways in question.

He then dug into the inside pocket of his tux jacket and pulled out another black box.

I knew that I loved him. I knew that I wanted to marry him. I knew that my life would never be as it was supposed to without him. But this little black box was like the proof that this all was real.

He opened it and I teared up at the sight. I looked at him and he was looking uneasy. As if I could dislike any ring he bought me. It was a gold chevron shaped ring and had diamonds in the chevron. It was unique and precious just like us.

He took it out of the box and I was surprised that the man who rescued me and loved me without fear was shaking as he placed the ring on my finger. I met him halfway and it fit just right. How he knew my ring size was a mystery.

I almost flew onto the other side of the blanket. I nearly knocked him over in my exuberance. I held onto his neck forever. I never wanted to let go of him. I wanted to knock him over and kiss him until my lips were numb, but we were on the beach and I wanted him all to myself.

I was in heaven as I had a ring, and not just any ring, on my finger and a beautiful bracelet on my arm. They could be made of straw and they would still be the most gorgeous things in the world.

"All the overtime?" I guessed.

"Yeah, it was so worth it." He shrugged like it was no big deal.

"You wanna stay here?" I asked.

"I don't care."

"Can we just go home?"

"Home where?"

"I only have one home."

He nodded and we headed to our home.

We got in and the apartment was empty. I ran into his room and yelled "I'm taking shorts and a shirt" as I grabbed them and ran into the bathroom. I took off those ankle-breaking, blister-making, awful shoes and padded barefoot back into the bedroom I shook my hair free of the clips that Rebecca had practically stabbed into my skull and took out the earrings too.

Carlos had already traded his tux for shorts and no shirt. He was in the kitchen making noise.

"Again?" I asked.

"Maybe," he shot back.

He came strolling in with two bowls. "Or maybe I was fixing your smart aleck mouth some ice cream." He bent down to give it to me and kissed my temple.

"Or that."

I was sitting sideways on the couch and he moved my legs up and sat under them.

"Ok, I gave you jewelry and I fed your ice cream. Now I need to talk to you about something serious."

"Are you saying that you buttered me up on purpose?" I put my bowl on the coffee table.

"Yup."

"Shameless."

"So the lease on this place ends at the end of the month and you will be gone the week before, to see your Dad. So, what I need to know is do you want to live here or should I start looking for a new apartment?"

"Awww, I like it here. This is our place. What about your brother?"

"He's going to live at another apartment complex with his friends."

"Well, a smaller place would be cheaper, right?"

He nodded and said, "Well, we have time. I just either have to be out by then or sign another lease for this apartment or a smaller one in the same complex."

He was playing with my bracelet, moving it back and forth on my wrist.

I loved that bracelet and even more I loved that new ring on my finger. I sat there for a few minutes working up the courage for what I wanted to do next. My face was blushing so furiously that my skin was tingling.

I took his bowl and put it next to mine. Caution and pure want battled each other on his face as I moved to straddle his legs and sit on his lap facing him.

He took a shaky breath and he was temporarily frozen in place at my showing of risqué behavior.

"What? You gave me my ring on a public beach. It was hardly the place for me to thank you…the way I wanted to." The roles were reversed and I was loving every minute of my newfound brazen self.

"Jenna," his breaths were choppy and nervous.

"Carlos...What did I ever do before you? I feel like I was just existing, walking around like a zombie. But now I live for the next time I can see you and hear you say my name and..."

The whole time he was staring at my lips and I couldn't contain myself anymore.

Apparently, neither could he.

He reached behind me and splayed his hands over my back as he pulled me as tight as he could to his chest without crushing me. Our lips collided at the same time and I scooted closer and closer until there was nothing between us. The burn started on my lips as they danced with his and blazed through the rest of my body.

His hands roamed under the hem of my shirt on each side of my waist. I gasped and broke free of the kiss. He had never let his hands wander. Not that I had a problem with it. He broke away abruptly.

"Are you staying here tonight?" He was still cautious and unsure.

"Yeah, I told her I wasn't coming home anytime soon."

He smiled brightly and lifted us both off of the couch and into his bedroom where he put me down on the bed and lay down next to me. I reached out for him to continue what I had started in the living room, but he pinned my arms down at my sides.

"J, please...I'm in hell trying to control myself here. Don't make it worse."

I groaned and said a pitiful 'Fine' and went to my side of the bed and he crawled over beside me and lay down. We faced each other breathing the same breaths. I needed to be nearer to him so I moved to lie on his chest and he chuckled knowing that he had won this round.

I fell asleep by the rhythm of his heart and my new ring being turned over and over on my finger.

The next morning I woke up about 7 and rolled out of bed barely conscious. Carlos reached out and grabbed my t shirt and said, "Where are you going? Are you ready to go hom....there?"

I went back to the bed and kissed him by his ear and said, "I'm going to make you breakfast. Go back to sleep."

"Mmmm, ok." He rolled over and was out like a light.

I went to the kitchen and made him French toast and bacon.

After I finished I went back into the bedroom and crawled into bed next to him and I screamed when he grabbed me and threw me on top of him.

"You were awake?" I gave him my best damsel in shock face.

"Yeah…I never went back to sleep. I was waiting for you to come back."

"Sneaky."

"You love me."

I leaned down right in his ear and said, "Remember that, Carlos, remember that I love you."

I got up and said, "Come on and eat."

Chapter 22

After breakfast Carlos brought me home. I consoled myself with the thought that there were only a few more days until graduation and then this chapter of my life would be over. He kissed me before I got out of the car and then cleared his throat when he saw my Mom in the window gawking like the voyeur that she was.

She looked pissed and Carlos saw it too.

"Are you going to be ok?" He asked while still staring at the window.

"Yeah..." I was trying to convince myself as much as I was him.

"Hey," he shook my hands trying to bring me out of my funk.

"Ok, call me if you need me, or want me or...just call." He was rambling.

"Yeah," I tried to smile... "It'll be fine." My face was getting hot, not from blush but from annoyance.

I got out of the car and opened the back to get my dress and Rebecca's shoes and purse and earrings out.

Carlos sped away as I walked towards Rebecca's house to return her things. She answered the door in a robe and holding a cup of coffee looking groggy but asked if I had a good time and I thanked her again for everything.

I walked into that blue house; it wasn't really home anymore and braced myself for the dual personality mother. I knew there would be words about the fact that I was still wearing his clothes and sporting a ring.

I reminded myself that I hadn't done anything wrong. I was just happy and in love and getting out from under their thumb. They hated the loss of control.

I made my way into the living room, all clear. As I passed through the hallway, trying to make it into my bedroom unscathed, I heard a clearing of Medusa's throat and I turned to face her. She was sitting on her bed and Wallace was sitting on his side puffing on one of his disgusting cigarettes.

She started up almost immediately, after giving me the dirtiest of dirty looks.

"So, you come home the morning after prom, wearing *his* clothes instead of your dress and..." She got up and zeroed her sights in on my ring.

"And flashing...what?...an engagement ring?"

"Yes."

"You know why girls get engaged at your age Jenna? I'm sure you do. We've noticed you getting a little chubby here lately. So...he knocked you up and now you're gonna get married and be so happy, right? How sweet."

I couldn't believe this was coming out of my mother's mouth. I mean, she had never thought the best things of me. And I knew that I was the bane of her existence, but I never knew she could think, much less say, those things about me. Why couldn't I get the regular Mom who was happy for me? I mean, I'm sure that thought would pass through any mother's mind at their teenage daughter getting engaged, but they didn't say it. Why did I get stuck with the Mom who always, automatically assumed the worst about me in every single situation? She stole from me, screamed at me, berated me, beat on me, made me loathe my own reflection in the mirror and now this? Wasn't all of the rest of it enough?

This is it. This is the end. They didn't deserve to hear how they had hurt me or how I felt like sometimes I would've been better off if I were never born. They deserved no explanation from me at all. So they got none. I nodded my head 'no' at my own question. They didn't deserve anything from me.

I turned and walked into my room and packed all of my stuff. May was asleep and I didn't want to disturb her. At this point, she probably wouldn't care. She was now a victim of their brainwashing and would have to decide for herself, like I had in this moment whether it was wrong or right. Whether it was the way she wanted to live, or like me, if she wanted to emerge.

I picked up my bags and took one last look at May. She would be treated better than me because she was their daughter and not just a product of a marriage gone wrong.

I passed their bedroom and paused for one second. They saw my bags then they looked at me and then turned their eyes back to the TV. I walked outside and called Carlos. He tried really, really hard to cover his happiness over the phone, but I could tell. He arrived shortly, almost as if he hadn't gotten very far away from my house.

I was not really looking forward to graduation, though I was looking forward to the events that I was trying to put into place after graduation. I knew what I needed to do and I was hoping against hope that all of the pieces would fall into place.

Graduation took forever, as there were about three thousand students or more all walking the stage. I had some honors, for good grades. Carlos had to work that day and it was held at seven at night, so he couldn't attend.

I sat there in complete boredom watching my fellow students walk the stage. They were all strangers to me and it was not because I didn't know them all. It was because there was what seemed like a football stadium worth of them. Finally, they got to my row and we got to get up and walk towards the stage. When I got up I nearly fell down because my butt was so numb.

My name was finally called and I could hear one set of hands clapping, one 'Wooo Hoooo!' over the crowd. Somehow he had gotten out of work and I loved him for showing up. It was nearly midnight by the time I made it through the herd and my parents were waiting with May by the door looking like they were late for an appointment and I was the hold-up.

They gave me a quick and cold 'Congratulations' and left abruptly. I don't understand why they even bothered.

I unzipped my gown and didn't even bother to find my cap. It was over, and thought most teenagers were ready to drag it out as long as possible; I was ready to get it done and get on with my life.

Natalie, Carlos' friend, brought me back to our apartment after graduation and I went straight to sleep. The next day was a Sunday and I didn't have anything to do other than pack my bag to go to Louisiana the next day. Carlos took the day off and I let him sleep until noon. We went to see a movie and went to eat but the silence that hung in the air was awful. We finally went back to the apartment and spent the rest of the day just holding on to each other. I was hiding my plan from him and my stomach was twisted in knots about it.

He didn't know it and I was probably really, really wrong to hide it from him. But this was the last time I would be in this apartment. This is the last time we would have this time here together. This was the place he had dubbed as our home. This was where we shared moments that anchored me to him.

The next day, I got my stuff packed and made my way towards the door for the last time. He was holding my bag in front of me.

I stopped walking and he turned around.

"What?" he said, the constriction in his voice was because he thought I was going to be gone for a week.

"I'm gonna miss you like I've never missed anything before." I said it as I looked at the floor.

He was against me in two strides. The meeting of our bodies and mouths was raw and rough and nearly on the brink of violence. He pressed me against the wall of the hallway by the front door and showed me how much he was going to miss me. His mouth left my lip and found my neck, the base of my throat and went a few inches lower than it ever had before. Tears ran the length of my face as he gave me his goodbye. His kiss retreated back to my lips and I thought I might never get enough of his body against mine. As if a switch had clicked in his head, he began his back down of what threatened to go too far.

Our mouths stayed touching, but not kissing, just breathing.

"Come back to me, Jenna. Come back and let me make you my wife."

"I love you so much. I would give anything to be your wife."

I wanted it. I wanted to be his wife and with him for the rest of my life and come hell or high water I was going to make it happen. But it was the 'come back' part that would never be.

Chapter 22

The LAX airport always made me feel like I was going to have a panic attack. Why they don't let people like me travel *inside* of their suitcase, I will never know.

The sight of it from the freeway, where you could see all of the planes and people coming and going, made it look like ants erupting from an ant hill.

Carlos had dropped me off at my Mom's house as she had my ticket and then they offered to bring me to the airport, which was weird, but Carlos had to go to work anyway. He had been taking a lot of time off because of me and couldn't miss any more. He had a hard time leaving the curb and I saw the beginnings of tears more than once. Why she wanted to drive me, I'll never know, but it was easier this way.

My Mom dropped me off at the curb. She had been pissed ever since I got back after prom night and had made an awful riot about my ring, but I didn't pay her any attention. I think she knew that she had lost, but that didn't mean she would stop trying. I had never tried to talk to them about everything they had done to me and how the scars felt like they would never heal. But one day, I was determined to make it known.

I tried to say goodbye to them and they didn't budge. Mom just gave me a half wave. I leaned over to May to kiss her and she looked out the window and refused to speak to me. She had gone to the dark side. After everything, I just had to let her go.

I got out and got my bag and went into the airport. I had flown home a couple of times, but this time was the last time.

I checked in and waited the excruciating time through the line to step into the security and the body scanner then I was on my way.

I waited until my seat was called and stepped into the plane. I hated the smell of planes. It smells like someone took regular air and pumped it through 'plastic smell' scented air freshener box and then pumped it back into the plane. I went through all the motions of seat belts and watching the flight attendant do her 'vogue' impression and let the plane take me away.

Before I knew it, I was in Memphis, catching my connection flight into Baton Rouge. I was riding on the moving walkway and I took a look out of the front of the airport and stared.

I could walk out of here right now. I could walk out and they would never know where I was. They wouldn't be able to find me if they tried. I could call Carlos and he could meet me here and we could start a life.

But again, it just didn't feel right.

I went to my next gate and while I waited I called him.

It barely even rang one time before he answered.

"I miss you already," he said.

I giggled. "You have no idea."

I told him about my thoughts of walking out of the airport and though I thought he would be upset, he understood. He said he had been thinking about us moving somewhere else, away from everyone. He had also been trying to find another job, a better one where he didn't work nights. I didn't even know about that, probably too wrapped up in my own garbage.

I got off of the phone after hearing that they were boarding the plane to Baton Rouge. He made me promise to call him when I got there.

I got into Baton Rouge about 9:15 that night. It was two hours ahead of California, so I knew that Carlos was at work, but tried anyway.

"You made it?"

"Yeah, are you at work?" I didn't want him to get in trouble.

"Yeah, I gotta go, but I'm ok now that I know you're safe. I love you."

"I love you. I'll call tomorrow." And I hung up.

My Dad, Step-Mom and Sophia were waiting for me as I came out of the gate exit. My Dad was a huge burly man who wore overalls. He stood about 6 foot 3 and towered over me and everyone else. My Step-Mom, I called her by her name, Marie, had strawberry blonde hair and was always cheery and kind.

Sophia was a doll. She had blonde hair like May's but it was finer and had more curl. It was on the top of her head like a fountain of blonde was cascading down to her scalp.

It was always awkward at first seeing them because I only got to see them once a year or so, but they had never been anything but nice to me.

My Dad knew about my mom, but never the full extent of her wrath. That would have to be remedied to make sure he knew how desperate I was.

We went back to their house and the next morning, I would begin.

The next morning I knew I was back in the South by the smell of biscuits and bacon. I fumbled out into the hallway and was told to sit down and eat.

They started asking me questions about school and future plans and I saw my window.

I didn't hold anything back. I told them about Mom and about my Step-Dad. I told them about May and I mostly told them about Carlos. I laid it all out like the twisted tale that it was and sat back and let it stew.

My Dad was the big silent type but you knew that when he opened his mouth to say something it was best if you opened your ears and listened well.

"I'm not even going to ask you why you never told us any of this. I know that you've always been kinda scared of your mother, but honestly I didn't think it was that bad. I thought a girl being with her mother was the best thing for you. I didn't know anything about taking care of a girl." He paused. "How serious is it with this boy?"

Marie thumped him and he corrected himself.

"Ok, man, I meant man."

I giggled at my big old Dad struggling with the fact that I was older and had to refer to my boyfriend as a man. I scooted my chair out and ran to get my engagement ring which I had stashed in my wallet on the plane. I didn't want to alarm them too much before I could tell the story.

I walked out and put my ring clad hand on the table.

Marie looked up and smiled and said, "Well, there you go."

Marie was a God-send and when my Dad went to work the next day, she stayed home with me and got the real story, the long version. She cried and laughed with me and asked me questions and was really interested and it seemed like she cared.

She got angry when she learned of things that I really hadn't paid attention to when I was growing up. Things like: I had never been to the dentist, ever. I had never been to a doctor since I was 16 and had a bleeding ulcer, which was courtesy of stress. Imagine that. I had never been allowed to get a driver's license because we would never have been able to afford another car and Mom was afraid I would do the kind of running around that she did when she was a teenager. I didn't even know nor have access to my social security number.

She patted my leg and smiled and looked at Sophie, who was watching the Lion King.

"I need to ask you a personal question Jenna, now don't get upset, ok?"

I had no clue what was coming next.

"Ok."

"Are you being safe?"

"Am I being safe doing wha....OH! Yeah, I am being safe by not doing anything unsafe."

"Ok, I get that. But we have to be prepared for things to get unsafe, yeah?"

"Just talk straight, ok?" I begged.

She giggled, "Ok, have you been to the gynecologist?"

"Ok, ok, never mind, can we go back to the jumbled talk?"

She laughed more and got up from the couch.

"Ok, I'm taking that as a 'no' and making you an appointment for this week. They can put you on some birth control...just in case."

I looked at Sophie who was playing with magnet letters while she sang 'Circle of Life' and said,

"Don't grow up Sophie, it's humiliating."

My Mom called my Dad's house that night and asked when I was coming to see her. She must have been in front of people because she was using that fake sweet voice.

I told her I didn't know when I was coming over. Dad and Marie had planned tons of stuff for us to do. She threatened me in a whisper over the phone, but I just hung up on her. I was done.

The rest of the week Marie made me go to the dentist, ugh, and the 'girl doctor', that's what we decided to call it.

Every day I called Carlos and I almost died from embarrassment when I told him about the 'girl doctor' part. He laughed and said, "That's probably smart Jenna." I changed the subject quickly, but not smoothly and he found that hilarious.

I missed him like I had lost one of my appendages.

I saw my Mom twice that week and made the visits under an hour. Marie drove me and when I called her she came and picked me up. After the second time she growled in fake anger, "We really need to get you a driver's license. This is the pits."

I wanted to talk to Dad and Marie so badly about my plans, but didn't know how to broach the subject.

The week had gone by fast and on that Sunday afternoon over dinner, I had planned to dive in head first. But then Marie very obviously kicked my Dad under the table and he put his fork down and started a discussion that would change my life.

"Jenna, Marie has been telling me what you two have been talking about all week. And we have been talking about how to help you and honestly, the way things stand I don't know how I can help you at all."

My resolve was broken and I sat at the table trying not to and failing at bawling my eyes out.

"Jenna, let me finish, ok?"

I nodded and he continued.

"Marie and I can't help you way over there in California. Your Mom, I think, no matter what you do, will always be over you terrorizing you. She has been making threatening calls and writing horrible letters to us for years."

My eyes bugged out of my head. She had left my Dad over ten years ago for my Step-Dad. Why would she do that?

"That being said, we want you to stay here. I know you have to think about it and I know that you probably have to talk to Carlos and that's fine. We will help you get settled here. You can get your driver's license, get a job or go to school or both, but the point is that you could be free to do what you want to here. And as long as you are doing something productive, we will help you."

Marie was holding my hand now and then it was her turn to talk.

"Jenna, think it over. And I know that you told me this week that it's hard for you to confront your mother. I know that's gotten easier for you lately but I have a plan if you want to stay here."

"What?" She had a devilish look about her and I needed to know the plan.

"Ok, all of you are supposed to get on a plane tomorrow right?"

"Right...." I dragged out the word trying to get her to tell me the rest.

"Easy. You are an adult. Don't get on the plane."

"She'll have a fit!" I gasped and laughed at the same time.

"Your Dad will stay home to intercept the phone calls and you're back in Louisiana, so if they try to come here, well, your Dad has a shot gun."

"I want to. Thank you and I want to stay....but..."

She read my mind.

"There's only one way to find out Jenna. Now go make the call."

I sat on my bed in my Dad's house for the longest time thinking of all the things I needed to say to Carlos and all the millions of ways he could break my heart in return. My brain and my heart were battling and my brain was winning. Tears were pumping out of my eyes faster than I could keep up.

I had tried to work so many plans in my head and none of them ever seemed right. They always felt wrong or like I was straying from the right path. This felt right. This was our shot to be together.

My dinner rolled the 'death roll' in my stomach and I ran to the bathroom and puked everything I had eaten.

I rinsed my mouth out and I went back to sitting on the bed trying to console myself.

My heart made one last, hopeful attempt to save me from myself.

I got a moment of calm and picked up the phone.

It rang and rang what seemed like an hour.

"Hello?" His voice calmed me, even if it may be the last time.

"Hey, I need to talk to you." I wasn't going to waste any time.

"Are you crying? What's wrong?" He was worried, he always was.

"I...I have something to tell you and I don't know what you're going to say."

"Tell me, J. You can tell me anything. You're kinda scaring me."

"My Dad thinks I should stay here, to get away from my Mom, for us to get away from my Mom. Dad and Marie said they would help me, and us, get jobs and me a driver's license and a place to live..."

He started spouting off questions.

"What does that mean? When? Are you staying there, or you're coming back and then leaving again?" I didn't recognize this tone. Was it aggravation or anxiousness?

"He thinks I should just not get on the plane tomorrow. He thinks it's the best way, a clean break."

I could hear him let out a breath and then nothing.

The silence was killing me. I could hear him shuffling around and then I could hear him pull out a chair. I could hear that telltale shoe tapping on the floor while I imagined his knee bobbing. It was our first phone conversation replayed again. And I felt like I did on that call. I was nervous and my stomach wanted to empty itself again.

This is it. I've ruined it. This is the end.

I started backtracking and making contingency plans. I would go back. I couldn't lose him. I could deal with my Mom as long as we were together. I could endure a lifetime of her terrorizing me if I had him to soothe me.

He cleared his throat and I was brought out of my emotional self-mutilation and planning in an instant.

"Jenna?"

"Yeah?" My voice broke as I said it.

Those few seconds of waiting were like watching sand siphon through an hourglass one grain at a time. The pain of waiting was almost too much to bear, until I heard his voice.

"I'm on my way."

Epilogue

I lay in the hospital bed and I was sore and exhausted. I closed my eyes for a split second when the door opened. He had the happiest smile and it was reserved for these moments. This was our third 'moment' but I knew that smile well.

He approached my bed and kissed me gently and moved some of my hair out of my face. I didn't have the energy.

"Jenna, she's gorgeous."

"I know. And she's loud."

"Yeah, she is." He laughed.

He was pacing the room, waiting and anxious.

The door opened again and a nurse poked her head into the door.

"Are you ready for her?" She looked like she was ready for me to have her.

"Of course." I sat up slowly.

She rolled in a see-through bassinette on top of a rolling cart. Those things are so weird.

The nurse left and Carlos reached in and took out our latest creation.

She was perfect and she was already sucking her thumb, but it didn't seem to be doing the job for her.

I got ready and put her to my chest to give her what she needed.

He sat next to me on the bed and we sat there in total joy and I reflected back on our lives.

We had come so far. We had been married for six years. We got married shortly after he arrived at my Dad's house. We had bought a house and were happy. Marriage took work, but it was not so bad after everything that we had already been through.

We had figured out some things along the way. We found out that those special cards and checks that May referred to were really credit cards that had been taken out in my name. There were also numerous other lines of credit and loans taken out in my name as well. We had spent years paying it all off.

I went to school, but never finished as our firstborn, a son, was only 2 pounds at birth and spent a good deal of time in the hospital and I stayed with him. By the time I wanted to go back I was pregnant with our second baby, a daughter who was a preemie too. Carlos went to school and finished.

This sweet little muffin in my arms was blessing number three.

Lily had fallen asleep and he took her from me but remained sitting by me.

He was an amazing father. He worked as hard, if not harder, than he did when we were in school and I still reveled in the touch of his calloused hands.

I looked at him holding her and the tears began again. It seemed like they had been flowing all day.

I touched her face and it was as soft as down. She nestled closer into her Daddy's chest and sighed. Like me, she had found her home in his arms.

I looked back to him and he was already looking at me.

"I love you, J," he said, and all I saw was the man who saved me from myself, who saved me from a life filled with hell and showed me pieces of heaven. Who held a broken soul and mended the cracks with love.

"I love you more. Remember that."

Emerge – Lila Felix

EMERGE PLAYLIST

JUILE JUNE /SILENT FILM

MEDUSA /BLACK COUNTRY COMMUNION

CHARMER /KINGS OF LEON

NURSERY ACADEMY /TOKYO POLICE CLUB

MMM MMM HE'S SO DREAMY /TALULAH GOSH

SOUTHERN GIRL /BETTER THAN EZRA

HOWL / FLORENCE + THE MACHINE

AWAKE MY SOUL / MUMFORD & SONS

TAKE ME HOME / MATT AND KIM

JUKE BOX LEAN / NEW BOMB TURKS

O'SISTER / CITY AND COLOUR

MINE'S NOT A HIGH HORSE / THE SHINS

NOW THAT I'VE FOUND YOU / PAUL MCDONALD

PLUMP / HOLE

Emerge – Lila Felix

NO ONE'S GONNA LOVE YOU MORE THAN I DO / BAND OF HORSES

COME CLOSER / MY MORNING JACKET

WEIGHTLESS / CITY AND COLOUR

ON CALL / KINGS OF LEON

THE FANTASY / 30 SECONDS TO MARS

COME UNDONE / DURAN DURAN

LULLABY / THE SPILL CANVAS

THE REVOLUTION IN ME / BLACK COUNTRY COMMUNION

SUCH GREAT HEIGHTS / IRON AND WINE

LAMPLIGHT / SILENT FILM

YOUR LOVE IS EXTRAVAGANT / THE ALMOST

Emerge –Lila Felix

Emerge - Lila Felix

Emerge —Lila Felix

Emerge ~Lila Felix

Emerge –Lila Felix

Made in the USA
Middletown, DE
04 April 2020